# DOLLARS OF DEATH

Determined to keep his past a secret from his wife and family, Frank Peters is forced to leave his beloved Hash Knife when the past catches up with him, before his men return from a cattle drive. He seeks the answer to a new life through the events of twenty years ago, but an old partner stalks the same trail for the dollars Frank seeks. With suspicions aroused when they return from the cattle drive Johnny Hines and Cap Millett ride the trail to the Dollars of Death, uncovering some strange happenings, as they attempt to save Frank from his past and preserve his future.

# DOLLARS OF DEATH

# DOLLARS OF DEATH

*by*

Jim Bowden

**Dales Large Print Books**
Long Preston, North Yorkshire,
BD23 4ND, England.

British Library Cataloguing in Publication Data.

Bowden, Jim
Dollars of death.

A catalogue record of this book is
available from the British Library

ISBN 978-1-84262-639-9 pbk

First published in Great Britain in 1979 by Robert Hale Limited



Published in Large Print 2008 by arrangement with
Mr W. D. Spence



Dales Large Print is an imprint of Library Magna Books Ltd.

Printed and bound in Great Britain by
T.J. (International) Ltd., Cornwall, PL28 8RW

## ONE

'I'm sorry, Mrs Fenton, but this has got to be the last warning. You have sharp words with Sloane, get him to toe the line or I can't be responsible for what might happen.' Jim Nolan, Sheriff of Benton spoke quietly but there was no mistaking the determined firmness in his words.

'But Sloane's harmless,' returned Lucy Fenton, brushing a wisp of grey hair from her forehead. Her voice was soft and her face, lined beyond its sixty years, wore a gentle smile.

'I've been telling you for the last four years to take the boy in hand, that if you didn't he might just grow up into a no-gooder.' At forty the sheriff's broad frame was beginning to hold a little surplus flesh adding to a size which, to Mrs Fenton, always seemed to fill this small room. 'Now he's around with this fella Concho Briggs, who drifted in here a couple of weeks ago, I'd say he was heading for trouble.'

'High spirits, Jim, high spirits, that's all it is. Sloane's not bad, never could be,' Mrs Fenton replied. 'I've been pleased of his lively company since my husband died four years ago. I'm mighty grateful to my sister and her husband for leaving Sloane with me when they went off to Texas. Don't worry about him, Jim, he'll be all right.'

'You met this here Concho Briggs?' asked Nolan. His opinion of Briggs was obvious from the tone of his question.

'Yes I have,' replied Lucy Fenton, emphasising her words in such a way that the sheriff knew her opinion differed from his. 'Sloane brought him to meet me last week, I always like to know who Sloane has for friends, and I might tell you, sheriff, that he was a pleasant young man.'

The sheriff raised his eyes to heaven. How gullible could she get? Of course Briggs would be nice to her. Couldn't she see through him?

'You've only seen one side of him,' Nolan insisted. 'I tell you he's no good, there's trouble brewing, I can smell it, so have a word with Sloane. I know he's not thoroughly bad but he'll be led on by this fella. A pity he didn't go to Texas with his folks, no disrespect to you Mrs Fenton, but he missed a father's steadying hand at a vital time. Released from it, his high spirits came out. They got a bit out of hand at times, now with Concho Briggs around they could lead him into trouble. So have a word: I can't be lenient any longer especially if he teams up with Briggs, besides, next sheriff could be a hard case.'

Mrs Fenton raised an eyebrow. 'Next sheriff? You aren't thinking of leaving, are you, Jim?'

'Well, it's not generally known, but yes I am. Sheriff's job at Pine Bluff is vacant. I've put in for it, better job than this one, and I'm told I stand a good chance of getting it.'

'Be sorry to see you go, Jim,' said Mrs Fenton, 'but best of luck, I hope you get it.'

'Thanks,' Nolan turned to the door, and, with his hand on the knob, looked back at the grey-haired lady. 'Just have a word with Sloane.'

Lucy nodded. 'Good day, sheriff.'

'Good day, m'am.'

As the door closed behind the lawman, Lucy Fenton sighed and picked up her sewing. Jim saw high spirits as badness. Sloane would be all right.

'Hi there, Charlie, heard the stage come in, had a good drive?' The bar-tender in the Dancing Girl greeted the short, stocky, leather-faced man who came to the bar.

'Yeah, thanks, Kane. Gave me a decent team in Hot Springs this time, not like the last when one horse went lame.' Charlie took the beer which the barman had drawn for him and drank half the glassful without stopping. As he put the glass down he wiped his lips with the back of his left hand. 'Ah, that's better, sure was ready for it. Seen Wally Price?'

'Ain't been in yet.'

'Need him next trip,' said Charlie casually.

'Something important?'

Charlie lowered his voice. 'Fifty thousand out of Hot Springs.'

Kane raised his eyebrows in surprise and, as he moved away to serve another customer at the far end of the bar, said, 'That sure merits taking Wally.'

As Charlie lifted his glass again he glanced in the mirror which ran the full length of the wall behind the bar. His eyes met those of a young man leaning on the mahogany counter a few feet from him. In almost the moment of meeting the young man's eyes turned away but Charlie felt sure they had been watching him.

The stage driver cursed to himself. He shouldn't have mentioned the cash but it had just slipped out. He knew Kane was all right and would keep his mouth shut but had this fella overheard? Charlie eased his conscience with another beer, taking it to a table to wait for Wally. Forget the young fella at the bar, stage would have Wally on it, best shotgun in the business in these parts.

In spite of reassuring himself, Charlie found himself studying the young man at the bar. Dark eyes lay in sunken sockets and moved with a shiftiness which, to Charlie, spoke of a mean streak, a characteristic accentuated by the thin lips and pointed chin. The light brown hair was thin and, when the man turned to go, he covered it with a dirt-stained battered Stetson which matched his well-worn clothes. There was a casualness about his walk as he crossed the saloon to the batwings but it did not fool Charlie. His years of experience had taught him to beware of such casualness, for more than likely there was a sharp alertness just below the surface which could be followed by the swiftest of movements whenever the necessity arose. Young as he looked, Charlie felt that the man, who left the batwings squeaking behind him, would not be one to meddle with.

Charlie pushed himself from the chair and went to the counter. 'Kane,' he called and indicated with an inclination of his head that he wanted a quiet word with him. 'That young fella that's just left, know him?'

'Stranger to these parts. Been in and out these last couple of weeks. You must have missed him.'

'Must have. Know his name?'

'Briggs, Concho Briggs.'

'Know anything about him?'

'No. I'm told young Sloane Wilkins knocks around with him but they've never been in here together, well, you know Sloane, never comes in here.'

'Reckon that Lucy Fenton's hatred of liquor, after it killed her old man, still exerts its influence.'

'Guess so.' The barman glanced in the direction of the batwings which had been pushed open to admit a well-built man of medium height. 'Here's Wally now.'

Charlie turned to greet the newcomer.

'Just the fella I want to see. Bring your beer to the table.'

Wally got his drink and joined Charlie. 'Guess it's a job,' he said as he sat down.

'Yeah, shotgun out of Hot Springs, day after tomorrow.'

Wally nodded. 'So I ride there on the stage tomorrow.'

'Sure.'

'Allowed to know what we'll be carrying?'

'Fifty thousand in notes, transfer between banks.'

Wally let out a low whistle. 'Sure hope no one gets wind of that.'

Wally's remark made Charlie feel uneasy about Concho Briggs again.

When Concho left the saloon he unhitched his horse and swung into the saddle. He turned the animal and rode at a walking pace along the dust roadway towards the row of white railings fronting the houses at the end of the main street.

When he neared them he saw a young

man repairing a pailing in front of the third house.

'Hi there, Sloane,' he called with an emphasised friendliness.

The young man looked up from his work and when he saw Concho's warm grin he returned it with a pleasure which danced in his brown eyes.

'Hi yourself, Concho.' Sloane straightened his broad back and rubbed his hands down his denim trousers which were tucked into the top of calf-length boots.

'Doing a neat job there,' commented Concho.

'Think so,' said Sloane, glancing at the repair. 'Thanks.'

'How about forgetting it for now and coming for a ride?'

Sloane's hesitation was only momentary. His grin widened. 'Sure thing, be with you in a minute.' He ran round to the back of the house where, a short distance away, stood a stable big enough for two horses. He saddled one quickly and led it to the street.

As he was climbing into the saddle, Concho suddenly yelled, 'Race you to the creek!'

'Hi you...' Sloane started to protest that he was not ready but, realising that Concho was already away and breaking into a fast gallop, he pulled his horse round, kicked it forward and with a loud yell set off after Concho.

The two riders pounded down the street sending anyone crossing the road scurrying for safety. Yell after yell broke from their lips in the exhilaration of the race. Then they were out of town and hooves tore at the grassland which stretched in wide, curving undulations for two miles, before dropping in a mile long gentle slope to the creek.

The hooves thrummed the tattoo of race across the earth and the two young men, wild with the excitement of the contested gallop, encouraged their animals to greater efforts with loud yells and whoops.

Concho held his distance over the first mile but by the end of the second Sloane had overhauled him and they tore towards the tree-lined creek neck and neck. Yelling and laughing neither could outride the other and they held their speed into the stream. Water splashed high soaking them both. With a whoop they were out on the opposite bank pulling hard on the reins bringing their horses into a quick turn and slowing them down. Breathing heavily, leaning on the saddle-horns, Sloane and Concho let their steaming mounts walk back across the stream. On the opposite side they slid from their saddles and lay full length on their backs drawing air deep into their lungs.

The moments passed as they lay staring at the deep blue sky through the gently swaying branches of the trees.

'Who's Wally Price?' Concho did not move as he put the question casually.

Though surprised by Concho's unexpected question, Sloane gave the answer automatically. 'Has a few acres just outside of town and does a few jobs for the stage-line, especially riding shotgun when necessary.'

'It's necessary day after tomorrow.' Concho's voice was quiet.

'Drive from Hot Springs.' The information followed naturally from Concho's facts. Then Sloane suddenly realised what Concho had said. He sat up sharply and stared at the still prone figure. 'What you mean, it's necessary?'

'Fifty thousand.' Concho had not bothered to look at Sloane. He wanted the words to make their own impact.

'Fifty thousand!' Sloane let go a low whistle. 'Hi, you joshing me? How do you know?'

'Fella named Charlie came into the saloon...'

'Stage driver.'

'Yeah, he was looking for Wally Price, and I heard him mention moving fifty thousand dollars from Hot Springs to the bank here.' Concho had directed his attention at Sloane and now he added casually, 'What say we take it?'

For one moment the question and the

implication behind it did not make themselves felt then suddenly they hit Sloane's mind. 'What! You must be joking?'

Concho sat up quickly and Sloane saw the fire of excitement in the dark eyes. 'Why not? We could do it.'

'Don't be a fool, Concho. With Wally Price riding shotgun.'

'He'll not pull the trigger if we get the drop on him first.'

'That won't be easy.'

'You know the route the stage takes,' pressed Concho, 'there must be some place where we could take it by surprise.'

'Sure,' agreed Sloane, 'but...'

'Well, there you are,' cut in Concho giving the impression that he thought it would be easy.

'But it'll bring the law on us,' Sloane protested.

Concho saw that it was not going to be easy to persuade Sloane to rob the stage for their own gain. 'Look, Sloane, I'm not thinking of keeping the money. We'd just hit the stage for the hell of it. Give this sleepy old town something to think about.'

'I dunno.' Sloane frowned and looked thoughtfully at the ground. 'Things might go wrong.'

'Naw, they won't if we plan it carefully. You know the country, so choose a good place to hide in for a couple of days and when we return to Benton with the money we'll be a couple of heroes.'

'Would be a bit of a laugh,' commented Sloane quietly.

Concho pressed home his persuasion on a weakening Sloane. 'You bet. We've had a few laughs this last fortnight, let's make this the big one.'

'It'll give Sheriff Nolan something to think about, maybe stop him getting at my aunt about me. He'll have to change his attitude when we ride in with the cash.' Sloane laughed loud as he imagined the situation – the sheriff apologising and eating humble pie while the townsfolk praised and lauded both himself and Concho as heroes for recovering the money. His eyes were alight and his lips quivered with excitement as he said, 'Right, we'll do it.'

'Good man,' cried Concho slapping Sloane on the shoulder. 'This sure is going to be some joke. Let's get planning. Where do we hit the stage?'

'Coyote Pass, four miles out of Hot Springs. No one would expect a stage to be held up so near town so I reckon Charlie and Wally will be less alert. Also it gives us a good chance to get away to the hills north of Hot Springs.'

'Good thinking, Sloane,' grinned Concho, already anticipating having fifty thousand dollars in his hands.

'I know the perfect place to hide. Found it by accident a couple of years ago. I lit off on my own for a few days. Aunt was nearly frantic when I got back.' He smiled at the memory. 'I reckon nobody had ever been there and probably no one's been since.'

'Great,' laughed Concho. 'Just great.' His mind was already seeing it as the ideal spot in which to take all the money for himself. If no one knew about this place a body could remain undiscovered for years, maybe never be found.

## TWO

The following morning Charlie checked the coach and horses while a youth, employed by the stage-line, kept them under control. He accepted mail for Hot Springs and, while three passengers got into the coach after saying goodbye to their friends and relatives, he secured it to the top of the vehicle.

As he turned to swing down to the sidewalk, Charlie paused and glanced across the street in the direction of the sheriff's office. Jim Nolan was leaning on the rail outside the office watching all the preparations for the stage run to Hot Springs. Charlie frowned. Outwardly he was the usual efficient stage driver but, beneath the surface, he was uneasy. He had spent a restless night recalling the eyes of Concho Briggs in the mirror in the saloon.

'Hi, Charlie, all ready?' Wally Price's lively voice broke into Charlie's thoughts.

'Yeah, yeah,' replied Charlie and he swung to the ground. 'Riding up top?'

'Guess I'll take the first half inside, catch up on a bit of sleep.' Wally climbed inside the coach and settled himself in the only corner seat left vacant.

Charlie went into the stage office for any last minute instructions and when he came out on to the sidewalk he hesitated, glanced across the street and called to the youngster holding the team, 'Hold 'em, boy, be back in a minute.'

Charlie stepped from the sidewalk and dust billowed away from his toes as he crossed the roadway.

'Hi, Charlie,' Sheriff Nolan smiled his greeting but that smile disappeared when he saw the serious expression on the wind-beaten face. 'Something troubling you?'

'Want you to do me a favour, Jim.'

'Sure, if I can,' said the sheriff.

'Will you ride watch on the stage tomorrow?'

Nolan was surprised by the request. Normally it would have come from the stage-line and not from the driver. 'From Hot Springs?'

'Yeah.'

'Carrying?'

'Yeah.'

'Figured so when I saw Wally Price going for the ride. Law in Hot Springs escorting you half way?'

'No. This is unofficial. Just me asking you a favour. Stage-line playing this shipment down even though it is fifty thousand. That amount slipped out when I was talking to Kane in the saloon.'

'He's all right; he won't talk.' The sheriff hastened to reassure Charlie.

'I know that but there was a young fella not far away and I couldn't be sure whether he overheard or not, but I got me an uneasy feeling. Can't ask the stage-line to change the shipment, it's got to be made tomorrow and they'd not take too kindly to me blabbing.'

'Know this fella?' Jim asked.

'Kane told me his name's Concho Briggs.'

'Briggs!'

'You know him?' Concern showed in Charlie's question when he saw the sheriff's reaction.

'Ain't a record as far as I can find out but he's a tearaway. I figure he'll end up a wrong 'un. Might just be fool enough to try to rob the stage. Sure, Charlie, I'll ride watch, better still I'll swear in three deputies and two of us will ride on each side of the trail. We'll keep out of sight, but don't worry we'll be there.'

'Thanks, Jim, I'm grateful,' said a relieved Charlie.

'Right. We won't come into Hot Springs, sheriff there might wonder why he's being kept out of the action. We'll pick you up at Coyote Pass.'

Sloane shivered and pulled the blanket tighter around his shoulders. He inched a little nearer the fire which Concho stirred into a brighter glow to heat their coffee and cook their beans.

Concho looked up and grinned. 'Cold, kid?' The last word was added with a touch of mockery.

'Hell, ain't you felt it?' spat Sloane.

'You'd be used to it if you'd roughed it like me.'

'Well, I ain't, and I don't reckon it's worth it just for the hell of holding up a stage.'

'You'll forget the rough night and the cold when you're Benton's hero. They'll talk about it for the rest of their days. Maybe they'll put a plaque up to you.'

'Knock it off,' rapped Sloane annoyed by Concho's tone. 'Doesn't seem worth it now, to take the money just to give it back.'

'Ho, careful now, you ain't thinking of taking the money for keeps?'

''Course not,' returned Sloane irritably. 'Just seems we're going to a lot of trouble and inconvenience to put a laugh over the folks in Benton.'

'You figured it would be worth it. You ain't

backing down, are you? You wouldn't walk out on your good friend Concho?' Sloane still looked glum. 'Aw c'm on, Sloane, you'll feel better when you've had a cup of hot coffee and the sun's driven the cold from your bones, things'll look different then.'

'Guess so,' muttered Sloane who wished the coffee would hurry up and boil and that the sun, which was merely paling the eastern sky, would shoot above the horizon and flood the earth with its warmth.

Two hours later, in the saddle above Coyote Pass, Sloane felt much better. He was warm inside, the sun had driven the cold away and now the excitement of the imminent hold-up was gripping him.

'How's this, Concho?' he asked.

'Fine, just fine.' Concho surveyed the pass for a few moments. 'I reckon near the start of the pass, just on that bend, it's sharp enough to slow the stage right down. There'll be no chance of the driver whipping his team into a fast getaway, and it'll be handy for us to break out of the pass quickly in the direction from which the stage has come.'

The two men eased their horses down the twisting path to the trail below.

Charlie checked the team's run down the gentle slope towards the narrowness of Coyote Pass. The pace slackened until the coach was moving between towering walls of rock towards a sharp bend in the trail.

Wally Price, cradling his rifle beside Charlie, half turned in his seat so that he could watch the rear of the coach. The driver called soothingly to the horses which were always restive in Coyote Pass but this route was two hours quicker than the trail flanking the hills.

Suddenly two horsemen, with Colts in their hands and bandanas covering half their faces, moved on to the trail a few yards in front of the coach. Charlie cursed as he automatically checked his team.

Wally swung round. He started to raise his rifle.

'Hold it!' yelled one of the riders.

Wally froze. He was caught. There was nothing he could do.

'Throw it down,' ordered the rider. The shotgun reluctantly pitched his rifle to the ground. 'Now your Colt, you too driver.'

As they did as they were told Charlie studied the man intently. Yes, he was sure – certain that this was the man he had seen in the Dancing Girl. That was the same battered Stetson. Concho Briggs. So if the sheriff was correct the other rider was probably Sloane Wilkins. Silly devil.

'Outside!' Sloane, at the door of the coach ordered the passengers out. They did so in sullen fear and obeyed instantly when he ordered them to lie face down on the ground. Sloane glanced at Concho who still had the two men on top of the coach covered.

'Give my partner the money,' called Concho. Charlie hesitated. 'Move!' There was no mistaking the threat if Charlie did not obey.

Charlie turned and unfastened the box and lowered it to Sloane.

'Up on top and lie face down. You first, driver,' ordered Concho.

As Charlie was scrambling on to the top of the coach, Sloane gave the lock on the box a sharp blow with the butt of his Colt. The lock broke, Sloane opened the box and in a matter of moments two bags of money were in his saddlebags and the box lay empty on the ground.

'All right,' Sloane called.

'Now you, on top.' Concho motioned with his gun at Wally.

The shotgun, alert for the slightest chance to get back at the hold-up men, knew he would have to make his move now or never, and he hated the idea of having his record of never losing a consignment spoiled. His right hand suddenly moved swiftly to a Colt which, whenever he was employed as shotgun, he placed on the seat beside him for emergency. His hand closed round it and swung the gun up.

There was a loud roar. Sloane started. Wally jerked and, driven backwards by the impact of the bullet, pitched to the ground besides Sloane's startled horse. As he steadied the animal Sloane stared in wide-eyed disbelief and horror at the blood flowing from the hole in Wally's chest.

Suddenly a flood of fear swept over him and showed in his eyes as he looked up at Concho. 'You fool!' he yelled. 'You bloody fool! You've killed him!' His mind was erupting in a wave of fright as it grasped at the consequences. The hold-up had turned sour. A bit of a laugh! Something to make Benton sit up! Return the money. They'd be heroes. Gone, all gone in one, damned, foolish squeezing of a trigger. Now the law would be after them for murder!

'Move! Move!' Concho's screaming voice pierced Sloane's bemused mind.

He saw Concho urging his horse past the stage. Sloane turned his mount and kicked it forward. They came out of the pass at a fast gallop and once up the slope turned north.

Sheriff Nolan, riding with his deputy on the north side of Coyote Pass, was moving closer to the edge of the heights to locate the coach when a shot boomed from the depths of the pass. He cast a startled look at his companion and urged his horse forward. He glanced across the pass to the heights on the opposite side and saw his other two deputies moving into a gallop. Jim Nolan was the first to reach the precipitous edge. He took in the scene in one swift glance and his horse had hardly stopped before he was urging it on, into a gallop which carried him on a course parallel to the two horsemen he had seen heading out of the pass. His deputy was alongside him and the two men on the opposite side of the pass, seeing the action of their sheriff, put their horses into a swift run in the same direction.

Hooves beat out a tattoo down a long incline and Nolan hoped he would gain on the two men who were riding hard up the ground which eventually levelled and merged with the slope down which he was galloping. He saw the robbers reach the level and turn their horses north.

'They're ours,' he yelled. He steadied his horse and signalled to the deputies on the other side of the pass to ride to the coach. With his signal acknowledged he settled into an earth-eating ride, attempting to overtake the riders ahead.

'What the hell did you do that for?' shouted a scared and angry Sloane.

'He pulled a gun!' yelled Concho.

'No cause to kill him. What now? We can't go back to Benton.'

'Never intended to!'

'What!' Sloane was shattered. Concho had strung him along and now they were condemned in the eyes of the law.

'Quit bellyaching and keep riding.'

Sloane was in a daze but kept his mount at a fast gallop by instinct. Earth flew beneath tearing hooves as they kept relentlessly on.

Topping a rise Sloane looked back. 'Hell!' He pulled hard on the reins bringing his horse to a sudden halt and turned the animal which, for a moment, fought against the pressure.

Startled by Sloane's action Concho checked his horse. 'What's…' His voice was cut short by Sloane's shout.

'They're on to us!' Fright showed on Sloane's face as he pointed at the two horsemen galloping towards them.

'Let's get to your hide-out!' yelled Concho and as one they wheeled their horses and set them into a gallop.

For a while they held their own but their horses were tiring and, as the hills steepened into mountainous country the pace slowed. Jim Nolan and his deputy gained steadily.

'Moon Pass – it's the only way for them,' called Jim when the mountains closed in on them.

'Let me have a crack with the rifle,' the deputy suggested.

'Soon. When they start that climb we'll shorten the distance quickly and you'll have a better chance.'

The lawmen pushed their panting horses on and, with the steepening ground ahead slowing Concho and Sloane, the gap between them shortened. A slight rise brought the lawmen into an advantageous position.

'Try it from here.' The sheriff halted his horse, drew his binoculars and focused on the fugitives as the deputy sought a suitable position from which to shoot.

'Briggs! Concho Briggs!' The sheriff gasped when he brought his binoculars on to the second rider. He moved his vision forward, feeling certain who he would see. 'The bloody fool! Sloane, you damned idiot!'

The deputy's rifle crashed.

Nolan saw Concho's horse rear and twist to fall sideways, sending its rider rolling down the slope.

'Shot!' yelled Nolan. 'C'm on.' He stabbed his horse forward.

'The other one,' shouted the deputy but Nolan was already on his way. The surprised deputy cursed, scrambled to his feet and ran to his horse.

The lawmen rode swiftly to the prone figure and pulled their horses to a sliding halt just as Concho, dazed and shaken by his fall, was managing to sit up. The sheriff and his deputy were out of the saddles and standing over Briggs covering him with their Colts.

'Jim, another shot?' queried the deputy.

Nolan glanced upwards at the still climbing figure. 'No, I reckon he'll come in.'

'But he ain't turned back.'

'Just automatic reaction, the urge for self-preservation, get away as far as possible from us but once he's at the top and thought things out I reckon Sloane Wilkins will give himself up, he's no criminal.'

'I dunno, bit risky for you if he doesn't.'

'He'll come.'

'I can make certain with one shot.'

'Too late.'

The deputy's lips tightened with annoyance. A huge outcrop of rock hid Wilkins from view and would do so until he was almost at the pass itself.

'Sloane! Sloane Wilkins! Sheriff Nolan here. We've got Concho. You ride into Benton with the cash and things will go easy with you!' The sheriff's shouts were tossed around the walls of rock and as they echoed from one to the other he knew Sloane would have heard.

Sloane reached the pass and, relieved to be alive, kept his horse moving. He shivered as he rode into the shadow of the towering faces of rock, and suddenly an overpowering feeling of utter loneliness and utter hopelessness swept over him. Utterly miserable he hunched himself in the saddle.

Only a short time ago he had felt free, life was good and he and Concho were going to have a bit of fun. Now he could be branded a killer along with Concho for he realised that no one could have seen who fired the shot. It would be his word against Concho's and, remembering how Concho had fooled him about taking the money back, he realised that Concho would say that Sloane had fired the shot. Sloane shivered again.

He recalled the sheriff's words. Go back? Like hell. He didn't trust such promises. The law would nail them both for Price's death. Maybe if he kept away they'd spare Concho for they couldn't be certain if he fired the shot. Forget Benton. Forget Arkansas. But where should he go? What should he do?

As he searched for a cleft in the rock face close to the opposite end of Moon Pass, Sloane toyed with his future. He could get right away. He had plenty of money. He shuddered. He saw Price's tumbling body, then oozing blood. 'No!' his mind cried out. 'Not that money, can't use it, not money with blood on it.'

Suddenly his attention was taken by the cleft he sought. He rode through its narrowness which opened on to a small flat plateau of rock the far side of which ended precipitously thirty feet above a boiling, foaming river which tumbled in profusion to a plunging fall.

Sloane stopped his horse and in miserable

dejection slid from the saddle to the ground where he lay, his body heaving in great sobs. Life had become a mess.

Suddenly Sloane started. He rolled over and sat up. Exhausted in mind and body he must have fallen asleep. He looked round. Only the roar of water broke the stillness of the secluded plateau. His horse stood quietly a short distance away. Sloane pushed himself to his feet. He knew what he was going to do. It seemed as if the solution had come to him in his sleep. He'd go to Texas and rejoin his family. No one down there would have heard of a stage holdup between Hot Springs and Benton in Arkansas. He'd tell his father the truth, change his name in case the law came looking and no doubt his family would stand by him and pass him off as a hired hand.

With his mind made up and a direction to go things didn't look so black. But he'd not use the money. He'd hide it here and forget it. Have nothing more to do with it. Tell no one about it and that would be an end to the matter.

Searching for a suitable hiding place he came to the edge of the plateau from where he could look back at the rock face clear down to the river. There he saw what he was looking for. The perfect hiding place. A ledge, about an arm's length down, let back into the rock face. Ideal.

Sloane hurried back to his horse and got the bags of money. Lying flat on his stomach he reached over and felt for the ledge. His probing fingers stretched, found it and examined. It would do. Carefully he lowered one bag and pressed it on to the ledge as far back into the rock face as he could. He dealt with the second bag in the same way, lay for a moment staring down at the foaming water, then pushed himself back from the edge and scrambled to his feet.

Cramming his Stetson on to his head he strode to his horse. He swung into the saddle and rode away from the plateau and a life he wanted to forget.

## THREE

Frank Peters straightened his broad shoulders from the post he was repairing, in the corral fence, a quarter of a mile from the ranch-house.

Martha would soon be calling him to the noon-day meal and he would be glad to get out of the hot Texas sun for a while. He wiped the sweat from his face as he stretched his stocky frame but his action froze into immobility when he saw the lone rider break the skyline and head towards the Hash Knife.

Johnny Hines! But even as the name of his foreman thundered into his mind he knew he was wrong, that it was a case of wishful thinking, wanting Johnny to be back from the cattle drive to Abilene, wanting to know if the drive had been a success, wanting the money to buy more cattle to add to the three hundred he had left and so build up a sizeable herd again. Even from this distance he knew that was not Johnny's sit of a horse.

The excited anticipation, sparked off by the first sight of the rider, drained from him and he leaned forward on the fence and watched the rider approach.

At first it was almost a disinterested appraisal. Probably some cowpoke looking for work. Well, he'd be disappointed. Frank had kept three men back from the drive and they were plenty to help him keep the ranch running until the rest of the outfit returned. He knew Johnny would pay them off in Abilene but he expected them all to drift back, they were a good crew, loyal to the Hash Knife.

Frank frowned. His brown eyes darkened with a puzzled look and his mind stirred, digging deep into the almost forgotten past. He found himself gripping the fence rail tightly. What had caused him to draw up dim memories? He sharpened his attention on the rider. He was still too far away to identify. The way he rode his horse … that was it! But who? When? Frank's mind tumbled back over the years. Then suddenly...

Concho! Concho Briggs!

Frank stiffened as the name bit deep into his mind, bringing anxiety and curiosity with it. Why the hell had this man come back into his life? Those early days had been almost forgotten, buried with a change of name and the respectability of owning the Hash Knife. He wanted nothing to disturb that. Only he knew about them. But now…?

It was Concho all right. No mistaking him as he rode nearer. The years had taken their toll but there was still that long face and pointed chin. A little thinner now, making the dark eyes seem to stare from sunken sockets more than they used to. The grin of recognition was still tight lipped.

'Howdy, Sloane,' Concho greeted as he halted his horse in front of Frank.

Frank nodded. 'Concho.' There was no warmth in this voice.

'Come on, Sloane, that ain't the way to greet an old friend who's been looking for you since he got out of jail five years ago.' Concho slid from the saddle. 'You should be glad to see me.'

'Why?' asked Frank testily, ignoring the outstretched hand.

Concho grinned and shrugged his shoulder. 'Just 'cos I'm an old buddy.'

'Well, I'm not,' rapped Frank. 'You can ride out right now! The past and Sloane Wilkins are dead. The present and Frank Peters are very much alive and you ain't gonna mix 'em.'

'Yeah, heard you'd changed your name...'

'Where did you hear that?' interrupted Frank. Suspicion and anger flashed from his eyes. He thought he had covered his tracks so that the past would never intrude on the present.

'Fella brought into jail had recognised you.' Concho was amused by the startled look which this statement brought from Frank. 'Figured you got away with it by changing your name? Well, I reckon you did or you'd have been picked up by the law. And don't get alarmed, this fella told no one else, said so just before he died but he figured as I should know seeing as how I was your partner.' Frank was relieved at this information but he made no comment. Concho wet his thick lips and wiped the hairy back of his hand across them. 'So I'm here to take up where we left off twenty years ago.'

'Like hell!' Frank's reaction was sharp and antagonistic. 'I told you that's all finished. I'm a respected rancher in these parts and that's how it stays.'

Concho spread his hands in acceptance and raised his eyebrows in agreement. 'Sure, sure Sloane…'

'Frank!' cut in Frank roughly.

'Sorry. Frank it'll be. I don't want to change anything. I didn't mean we'd go back to the old life. No, I just want my cut, my share with interest, of course, seeing you appear to have done well with it.'

Frank stared at Concho. 'You think I've

built this ranch up and got where I have from the money we took from the stage?'

'Sure.'

'Well, you're wrong. I ain't touched a penny of that money.'

Concho laughed in disbelief. 'Aw, come on, Sl... Frank. You don't expect me to believe you got this spread without it.'

'I sure did.'

'What do you take me for, a fool?'

'No. But it's right.'

The humour went out of Concho's eyes and left a suspicious disbelief in its place. 'Frank, you gotta be kidding.'

'I ain't. Sure, I was carrying the money as you well know but I got rid of it.'

'You what!' Concho's disbelief strengthened.

'I made it to the hills. Turned to wait for you, saw your horse go down and the posse take you. Two riders came on after me but I had a good lead and soon lost 'em in the hills. That night I got to figuring that the cash had blood on it seeing you'd killed the guard, so I wanted nothing more to do with it. Figured on turning it in but then I reckoned that'd be too risky. If they took me as well we'd probably both get strung up whereas, with only one of us in custody and no proof who fired the shot, you'd probably just get a jail sentence. Seems I was right.'

'You figured it right well, but I've had fifteen years of jail hell while you've had all that time free, so I want some mighty good interest.' Concho's mind had been racing over the possibilities and already he was beginning to see a situation which might be turned to his advantage. 'And don't josh me, Frank. I want mine and plenty more. This would be a nice place to settle down. We agreed to share fifty-fifty, so why not now. I reckon you owe me that much after all my years in jail.'

'Not with this ranch I don't,' rapped Frank angrily. 'I earned this with my own sweat and blood.'

Concho's eyes narrowed. 'Don't play games with me, Frank.'

'I'm playing no game. After seeing you arrested I figured I'd straighten my life out or I'd end up like you. Came south, took a new name, worked on a few ranches, saved my money and...'

'Added to that from the stage,' cut in Concho.

'Like hell.'

'You didn't get enough for this spread from cow-poke pay,' sneered Concho.

'No. I got lucky at cards and dice, saved it and after a while had a nice tidy sum.'

Concho looked at Frank suspiciously. He still didn't believe him. It sounded too far fetched when Frank had the stage money and could easily have used it.

'Nobody in his right mind would throw up the cash you had.'

'Well I did.'

'All right, prove it!' demanded Concho. 'Tell me where it is.'

Frank laughed. 'Take me for a fool? The law has a long memory. Concho Briggs is seen splashing money around, the law might just come asking questions and Concho might just talk.'

Concho's eyes darkened with anger. 'And I might just do that now. The law might like to know who the respectable Mister Frank Peters really is.'

Frank's lips tightened. 'You ain't blackmailing me. If you go to the law you'll never find out where the money is. As long as I hold the secret you'll never dare make that move.'

Concho stabbed at Frank's chest with his fore-finger as he glared deep into Frank's eyes. 'You owe me, Frank, you owe me. Just think it over. I'll be back.' He swung on his heel, reached for the saddle horn and swung on to the horse's back. He glared down at Frank. 'Just work out a partnership or things'll get rough.'

He swung his horse sharply and left Frank staring at his back and cursing the unexpected intrusion of the past.

# FOUR

'Frank! Frank! It's ready.'

The shout interrupted Frank's thoughts. He straightened from the fence, waved to his wife and set off towards the ranch-house.

Martha watched him for a few moments then swung off the veranda and walked to meet him. Frank's attention was taken away from Concho. He admired his wife's trim figure accentuated by the tight-waisted, patterned frock. She had kept her young looks even though she was forty and had suffered the trials of a rancher's wife with two daughters on the verge of womanhood. It hadn't been easy helping Frank build up the ranch and raise two children but now things were good–

Frank's thoughts came to a jolting halt.

Their peaceful, settled life had just received a stab – Concho Briggs had reappeared. The past, about which Martha knew nothing, had reared its ugly head. Frank frowned. Martha must never know. He'd do anything to keep it from her, do anything to preserve her happiness. Nothing would be too much for that. He loved her deeply and now they were reaping the benefit of the hard years and would continue to do especially if Johnny Hines had got a good price for the herd in Abilene. He'd promised himself he would make things easier for Martha, but now Concho–

Damn Concho! Frank's thoughts burst. He'd see Concho in hell first before he'd let him upset Martha's happiness. But what was the way out? The simple thing would be to tell him where the money was and let him have it but he couldn't see that as a final solution. As he'd told Concho there was a danger that he would give him away. Concho believed he'd used the money taken from the stage. Well, let him think that and cut him in as a partner in the Hash Knife. But, if he did so life would never be the same again. The shadow of the past would always lie across their lives. He would never know if Concho would talk, if, either deliberately or by accident, he would reveal everything to Martha. No, he would not have everything he had worked for threatened by Concho's presence. Besides Concho and he had never really been close friends, just a couple of youngsters who ran wild for a short while and really only held up the stage for the thrill of it. But Concho had to go and shoot the guard. Fool him. Well he'd paid but there was no reason for him to expect Frank to pay as well. Concho had threatened to be back, how was he going to hold him off?

'Hello, love.' The words cut into his thoughts. He started and was aware that his wife was near.

'Hi.' Frank forced a smile. He held out his hand. As Martha took it he pulled her to him, drew her close and, with his other arm, held her tight, holding on to the very life he regarded as precious, determining never to let anything or anyone spoil it. As he relaxed his hold he bent forward and kissed her. 'I love you,' he whispered, 'and always will, no matter what.'

A little surprised at Frank's actions out here in the open, Martha eased herself from his hold and looked questioningly at him with a teasing light in her deep blue eyes. 'And what's brought this on?' she asked, inclining her head to one side sending her light brown hair shivering across her shoulder.

'You,' replied Frank.

'Thank you,' she said turning and matching her step to his as they started towards the house. 'That's a nice compliment.' Martha had seen the disturbed worried look deep in Frank's eyes before he hid it. She was about to question him but then decided not to. Frank would tell her in his own good time. 'I came out to call you before but saw you talking to someone. Who was he?'

'Just some cowpoke looking for work.'

'Oh. Take him on?'

'No. We didn't need anyone. Johnny and the boys will be back.'

'You reckon all of them?'

'Sure. They're Texans and they know they've a steady job with me.'

The conversation had drifted away from the man to whom Frank had been talking. Martha felt sure her husband was holding something back and she reckoned that the troubled look, she had detected in his eyes, had something to do with the stranger. When she had first come on to the veranda to call Frank they seemed to be in a conversation which was more than query about a job and she had been concerned when the man appeared to threaten Frank. She wished Frank would tell her but if he didn't want to talk about it now she knew better than to pursue it. Martha was worried, she didn't like to see Frank bottling something up. She knew him too well and knew that it was unlike Frank to do so. But she would bide her time before she probed.

When they entered the ranch-house, their two daughters who had watched for them coming, had the food on the table and soon all four of them were enjoying the meal. As Frank glanced at them he became all the more determined that nothing should spoil this life they had.

Concho Briggs rode the ten miles to Cameron at a steady pace. There was no need for rush, no sense in straining his horse in this heat. Sure, he could use a cool beer right now but it would keep. He had his thoughts, and they weren't directed kindly at the man he had just left.

Frank had made it clear that he wanted none of the past. Concho cursed him for the brush-off. But Frank would pay, he'd see to that. He wasn't going to get away with using the stage money to set himself up and then ignore him.

Concho frowned. Frank said he hadn't used the money, it was still hidden but was he telling the truth? Concho was doubtful, yet he couldn't be sure. No matter, he was going to get what he reckoned was his and more. He'd let the clever Mister Peters see who was boss of the situation. The first thing he would move in on would be that spread. If the stage money had been used to set that up then he reckoned he'd be getting his due and if it hadn't, then he might flush Frank into disclosing where he had hidden it twenty years ago.

Concho smiled to himself. Things were going to go his way. Frank was going to be in for some surprises.

The two men crossing the dust roadway to the bank registered the only movement in Cameron. The rest of the small town sought shelter from the hot sun. Dust stirred reluctantly under his horse's hooves until Concho brought it to a halt. He swung from the saddle, stretched and climbed on to the sidewalk. The batwings squeaked behind him as he crossed the floor of the Gilded Cage to the long counter. He called for a beer, drained the glass as soon as he had it, asked for another, picked it up and went to a corner table occupied by two men.

'How'd it go?' said one, eyeing Concho from grey, cold eyes as he sat down.

'Didn't want to know me.'

'What!' Concho's announcement brought a startled reaction from the two men. From their lolling casual attitude they sat upright, staring with surprise across the table at Concho.

'Take it easy, take it easy,' soothed Concho. 'It ain't as bad as it sounds.' He leaned forward and lowered his voice. 'There can be big pickings, maybe bigger than we first thought, if you still want in on it.' Concho looked questioningly at the man who had spoken to him when he had arrived. 'Wade?'

The thin mouth above a receding chin had a meanness which did not disappear when the lips parted in a grin which revealed stained teeth. 'Sure, sounds as if you've cottoned on to something better than we'd hoped for. Tell me more.' The enthusiasm of his words did not warm his tone nor did they bring life to the greyness of the eyes which watched Concho closely.

Concho nodded and turned to the other man who in contrast to his companions was short and stocky with a square, angular jaw and round cheeks which seemed to narrow his eyes into slits so that it was hard to see his reactions in them. 'Ed?'

'I want to turn that ride from the pen into something,' replied Ed. 'What did that old sidekick of yours think of the idea of using his ranch for our lucrative activities?'

'Didn't get a chance to mention that – well I figured it best not to when I saw his first reaction.'

'Not pleased to see an old friend?' queried Wade.

'You'd have thought I was the devil himself. Didn't want to know. Told me to get, didn't want his nice little set-up spoiling by the past.'

'But what about your share of the money from the stage?' asked Ed.

'Figure he didn't owe me 'cos he'd never

used it.'

'What?' Wade and Ed exchanged surprised glances and then stared at Concho wanting an explanation.

'I see you're like me don't believe him.'

Wade shrugged his shoulders. 'Would any man?'

'Right.'

'So what you got in mind, Concho?' asked Ed.

'Well, I got to figuring as I rode back here. First, the bastard's going to pay and pay heavily. If he used the money for the ranch then I want my share, if he didn't...'

'If he didn't,' interrupted Ed, 'why didn't he tell you where it was and let you pick it up?'

'He figures if he did that I might get careless and talk and the past would catch up with him. He doesn't want his reputation around here spoiling. He's straight now. The past and those in it went when he changed his name.'

'You could still tell the law...'

'Come off it, Ed, do that and we've spoiled our chances,' cut in Wade.

'Guess so,' agreed Ed, making a quick assessment of the situation.

'Right, but I figure there's someone we might be able to use as a threat to Frank,' revealed Concho. 'We were about a quarter of a mile from the house, Frank was repairing a fence, but I caught sight of a woman come on to the veranda.'

'Wife?' queried Wade.

'Don't know. I didn't let on I'd seen her. But I'll find out. Whoever she is I figure she's one of the reasons Frank wants his past keeping quiet.'

'You mean threaten to tell her and Frank'll see things your way,' commented Wade.

Concho grinned. 'You catch on fast.'

'He'll have to cut us in,' grinned Ed.

'Maybe more than that,' Concho returned the grin with a knowing wink. 'Clever Mister Peters is going to pay.'

The following morning Concho drew the clerk of the Cattlemen's Hotel into a casual but revealing conversation which sent him hurrying to the café where Wade and Ed were having breakfast.

'What's pleased you?' asked Ed, reading the look on Concho's thin face.

'Just learned two things which we can put to use. Frank's married with two daughters and all except three of the Hash Knife outfit took a herd to Abilene. And those three are away in the hills after mustangs, likely to be there another week. Wondered why the ranch seemed quiet.'

'Then we've got a great chance to move in,' grinned Wade.

Concho laughed. 'Lady Luck's sure smiling on us. Now let's make a few plans.'

As they ate their breakfast the three men discussed their tactics.

It was nearing noon again when Frank saw three riders approaching. The excitement that it might be his foreman returning from Abilene was missing today for Frank had the encounter of yesterday in his mind. The threatening words which Concho had left had troubled him. Concho's ride was instantly recognisable today.

Frank cursed. He laid down his hammer and hitched his gun belt to ease it more comfortably on his hips. It was an automatic reaction as he sensed danger. Frank frowned and spat disgustedly in the dust. What the hell was he thinking of? He was outnumbered three to one. He hadn't a chance, he was no gunman. Useful with a Colt but not so used to gunplay that he could outshoot three. Try anything and Martha would be a widow. But he was damned if he'd back down to Concho and yet he sensed an impending, hopeless position.

'Howdy, Frank,' Concho greeted amiably. 'Hope you're in a better mood today 'cos I brought a couple of pals along, Wade Costain and Ed Farnham.'

The two men nodded but Frank only acknowledged them with a glance.

'I hope you've thought over what I said yesterday,' remarked Concho swinging from his horse. As he turned to face Frank, Wade and Ed slid to the ground.

'Answer's the same,' replied Frank coldly. 'So I'll be obliged if you'd all ride on.'

'Aw, come on, Frank, I thought you'd view things differently today. I realised it must have been a shock to see me yesterday so I figured when you'd had time to think things over you'd want to put things right by me.'

Frank was aware that as Concho had been speaking Wade and Ed had casually moved on either side of him against the fence.

'Thought you said this fella was a friend of yours,' remarked Ed.

'He is, he is,' commented Concho. He grinned at Frank and slapped him in the front of his shoulder. 'Aren't you, Frank?'

Frank's eyes narrowed. He scowled, showing his annoyance. He realised the threat behind the supposed friendliness of the sharp blow.

'I don't owe you, so git,' snarled Frank.

'Oh, getting angry,' said Wade in mock amusement. 'Now that ain't the attitude to adopt to our good friend, Concho. He figured that given the money you owe him he'd put it with yours and then us four could operate this here ranch very nicely.'

Frank glared at Wade. 'Like hell!' His voice was vicious. 'The Hash Knife is mine and mine it stays. Concho has no right to any part of it.'

'Forgetting the small matter of a stage hold-up and the money you took?' said Concho. His voice was quiet but there was a hidden menace in its smoothness.

'I told you yesterday I hid that money and I ain't ever been back.'

'In that case tell Concho where it is,' hissed Ed close to Frank's ear.

'And risk the law catching on,' said Frank.

'Suppose we tell who Frank Peters really is,' said Concho.

'You won't tell the law, that way you get no money and…'

Concho's laugh cut into Frank's words. 'Not the law, Frank, as you say that would be foolish but telling your wife and daughters, that would be a different matter.'

Frank stiffened. His eyes blazed with anger at the threat of the past being revealed to Martha.

Concho grinned. 'I see I figured right. I wasn't sure whether your wife knew about your past, now I see from your eyes she doesn't.' He turned to his horse. 'I guess she'll be mighty interested.'

Frank started forward but found himself pushed back hard against the fence by Wade and Ed. Concho swung into the saddle and from his new found height grinned down at Frank. 'She might as well know right away.' He started to turn his horse.

'Hold it,' gasped Frank. Concho halted his mount. 'Climb down. We'll talk.'

'That's better, isn't it boys?' grinned Concho.

'Sure is,' smiled Wade.

'I knew you'd see reason,' said Ed.

Concho moved from his horse to stand in front of Frank. 'Well?' he asked.

Frank licked his dry lips. His dark frown

showed his annoyance at being caught in this situation. 'If I tell you where the money is will you ride out of here and never return?'

'Well, now that's a change,' said Concho. 'Thought you were frightened the law might pick Concho Briggs up if they realised he was spending a lot of money and that Concho might talk under pressure.'

'That's a risk seems I'll have to take,' rapped Frank. 'But I want your word you'll never come back here.'

'Well – I can't rightly be sure about that, can you, boys?'

'No,' replied Wade and Ed. 'In fact,' Wade went on, 'I was just figuring I might stay around here.'

Startled, Frank glared angrily at him. 'Like hell,' he snapped, 'you ride out of here for that money and don't come back.'

'Frank,' said Concho smoothly, drawing the rancher's attention back to him. 'I reckon Wade ain't thinking of the money. I figure he's maybe thinking like Ed and me … the ranch.'

For one split moment the words did not seem to register and then as they did Frank almost exploded. 'The ranch!' He started forward but Ed and Wade pulled him back hard against the wood. A new alertness had come to them. The time had come to stop messing around.

'You hear Concho out,' rapped Wade.

Frank realised this demand had all been cut and dried before these three had ever reached the Hash Knife. It had been their intention all along to move in one way or another.

'I figure you owe me my share of the money plus fifteen years interest, so I'll take the ranch instead. Like you said, Concho Briggs with a lot of money might bring the law sniffing around.'

'Give you what I've spent most of my life working for!' gasped Frank.

'No, Frank, not give, a payment of a just debt.'

Frank's lips tightened. His mind pounded under the implications of the suggestion.

Lose all he had worked for. See a dream shattered in a few seconds. Where would he go? What would he do? Desperate situations draw desperate actions. His hand moved fast, closed round the butt of his Colt and started to draw it from its leather. But his position was hopeless. A fierce grip clamped on his wrist.

'That would be foolish!' hissed Wade.

Frank stiffened then slowly relaxed his hold on his Colt.

'That's better,' approved Wade, who released his grip on Frank's wrist and removed the Colt from its holster. He emptied the chamber of its bullets and slammed the gun back into its leather.

'Well, Frank, have I to take a ride to your house?' quizzed Concho.

'What do you figure my outfit's going to do? You'll hardly be out of sight and I'll have them after you.' A note of assurance had crept back into Frank's voice as he seized on a straw to try to outwit these men.

Concho laughed. 'You're going to be

mighty clever. Going to conjure them out of nothing?' His face clouded with annoyance. 'Quit stalling! You ain't got a man on the place. Most of them are up north with your herd and the three you kept back from the drive are out mustanging.'

Frustration gripped Frank. Concho had done a thorough check. He held all the cards. 'What am I going to tell my family? It's going to look strange if I walk in and say we're leaving. They know how I've worked to get this spread and to suddenly throw it all up– Besides, Martha's figured on us being here for the rest of our lives.'

'You'll think of something,' replied Concho. 'Tell you what, say you sold out for a good price too good to turn down.'

'There'll be no money to show for it,' pointed out Frank.

'Apparently you have only one secret from your wife – your past. Well, there sure can be some money – you can have my share of the stage money!'

'I'm not touching that,' rapped Frank.

'That's up to you. If you can explain why no money changed hands then you needn't bother, but if not – well there it is if you want it.'

Frank sighed. He was cornered. There was no way out. Unless he told Martha about his past. But even that wouldn't solve matters for Concho and his two side-kicks would still muscle in on the Hash Knife. 'When do you want me out?'

'Tomorrow.'

'Hell, give me time.'

'Tomorrow. In fact we'll stay now. You can introduce me as the new owner and Wade and Ed as my partners.'

Frank hesitated. He glanced round the three men and knew from their stares that it was hopeless to go against them. He pushed himself from the fence and walked to his horse, scanning the skyline of the hill to the north. What would he give to see the Hash Knife riders breaking that skyline now? But not a movement marred the sharpness of the hill. He unhitched his horse from the fence, climbed into the saddle and turned to find Concho and his side-kicks already mounted.

The four men sent their horses in the direction of the ranch-house.

## FIVE

A troubled look came to the pleasant, open face when Martha glanced out of the window and saw three men accompanying her husband to the house. Her immediate reaction was of dislike for them and a feeling of foreboding gripped her.

She felt sure one of them was the man whom she had seen talking to Frank yesterday. He had been too far away for her to study his features but he wore the same shirt and the stetson was tipped slightly forward.

Frank had been strangely quiet ever since that meeting yesterday. He had denied that something was worrying him but Martha knew differently. She hadn't been married to him for nineteen years without getting to know his various moods. Yesterday he was worried and didn't want to share the problem with her yet previously they had never held anything back from each other. It hurt Martha to think that for the first time her husband had not confided in her, that he had not looked for her help when it was needed.

If this was the same man who had only been looking for work why had he returned with two other men?

Martha went out on to the veranda. The riders were near and she saw the change of expression on Frank's face when she appeared. It was as if he was forcing himself to be pleasant, as if he was making an effort to banish the gloom she saw in his face the instant she stepped outside. That gloom must have been put there by these three men and he was trying to keep it from her.

'Hi, honey,' he called as the four riders pulled to a halt in front of the house. 'Can you manage three more for food?'

'Yes,' Martha replied but Frank saw the look of annoyance which she shot at him, which was strange for Martha for she was always willing to sit another at their table. Frank knew from her reaction that she did not like the three men with him. He groaned inwardly. This wasn't going to make things any easier.

The men swung from their saddles and tied their horses to the rail. As they came to the veranda Frank performed the unpleasant task of introducing them.

'Martha this here's Concho Briggs, Wade Costain and Ed Farnham.'

'Howdy m'am,' they each greeted in turn which Martha returned with a mere nod of the head.

Frank decided to come straight to the point, it was no good postponing the agony, better to get it over and done with.

'Martha, I've sold the ranch to Mr Briggs.' The words sounded unreal as if they were echoing from a dream and carried no meaning. It was only when Martha spoke that the full meaning of what he had said hit him.

'What!' Martha was stunned. Her eyes widened in disbelief. 'You can't!'

'He offered me a price I couldn't refuse.'

'But it's our home!' protested Martha. Her face had gone chalk white. She felt numb inside as if she wasn't there and yet her mind was clear and sharp and she knew she had heard right.

'Yes, I know, but we'll find another.'

'I like it here.'

'Honey, we…'

'You knew I wanted to spend the rest of my days here.' Tears welled in Martha's eyes. 'Just when we've got everything as we wanted and Johnny soon coming back with…' The words caught in her throat. She clenched her fist and held it to her mouth as if trying to stop the flood of tears which suddenly burst from her eyes. She turned and with sobs racking her body, ran into the house.

Frank's heart ached for her. He wanted to reach out and hold her, to comfort her and tell her everything would be all right but she was gone. He turned slowly to face the three men.

'You bastards,' he hissed. Venom spat with

the words. His eyes filled with hatred. 'I'll get you one day for this, so help me God.'

Concho grinned. He stepped forward and patted Frank on the shoulder but Frank pulled himself away as Concho spoke. 'You won't,' he said quietly, 'or you know what will happen. Don't take it too hard, Frank. Tell you what, we'll spare you something, we had figured on staying but it'll look better if we go, besides you'll have the little lady all on your own, give you time to put things right with her. But first let us have a document signing the ranch over to us.'

Frank shrugged his shoulders and let the three men into the house. He found some paper and a pen and started to write.

'Hold it, Frank.' Concho stopped him. Frank straightened and looked at Concho, hostility smouldered in his eyes. 'I reckon you can add the cash that's coming from the sale of your cattle in Abilene.'

'What!' Frank's eyes widened with disbelief. 'Not that! I need it.'

'Write it in!' ordered Concho.

'But I'll be broke,' protested Frank.

'Too bad.'

Frank stared at Concho. His lips tightened as he controlled his desire to smash the grin off Concho's face.

'Want me to call your wife?' Concho's question was a threat.

Frank turned back to the sheet of paper and started to write.

When he had finished he signed the statement and handed the paper to Concho to read it through.

'Fine,' he said. 'Glad you saw things sensibly.' He glanced at Wade and Ed. 'That's settled so let's ride for town.'

Frank followed the three men on to the veranda and fumed with helplessness as they unhitched their mounts and climbed into the saddles.

Concho checked his horse. 'We'll be back at noon tomorrow, we want you gone!' He turned the animal and rode away followed by Wade and Ed who both nodded at Frank with satisfied grins.

Frank was tense with rage. He almost turned into the house for his rifle but the thin line of reason did not break and that held him back. Killing wouldn't solve anything. He'd have three dead men to explain away. Besides, he was no killer, although he'd been driven to the brink of becoming one.

As some sort of calmness took over he turned reluctantly to the house. How could he explain to Martha? What could he say to try to put her broken dreams together?

He looked in the room to the right of the front door but she was not there. As he made his way to the kitchen he heard sobs coming from the bedroom. He hesitated beside the closed door, then took a deep breath, as if trying to draw strength for the ordeal which faced him, and pushed the door open gently.

Martha was lying face downwards on the bed, her head in the pillows, while sobs shook her body. Frank, his heart aching because of the hurt he had caused the woman he loved, crossed the room and sat down on the bed beside his wife. He laid a hand gently on her shoulders.

'I'm sorry, Martha,' he said softly. 'I should have broken the news more gently.'

For a moment she said nothing then her voice muffled by the pillows, came with a cry of anguish. 'Why, Frank, why?'

'I was offered a price I couldn't refuse.' He waited. Martha said nothing so he added. 'Please try and understand.'

Martha turned over slowly and looked hard and long at her husband through tear-stained eyes. She did not speak. She waited for him to go on. She knew there was more to his action than price. Her heart cried out for him to tell her but Frank just gazed at her with eyes pleading for her to accept what he had done.

Martha's sobs stopped, though tears still flowed. She bit her lips, trying to master the sadness and the hurt.

'Frank.' Her voice was quiet and low. 'You haven't told me everything.'

'It was a good offer,' Frank said but Martha recognised the words held no conviction. Something was eating at her husband. Her heart went out to him. She wanted to help but more than anything else she wanted his trust.

'Those men aren't ranchers, they weren't cattlemen, they're not your type. Why should they turn up out of the blue and make an offer for the ranch? One of them was the man who visited you yesterday, the man whom you said was looking for a job, now he's here again today and is buying the ranch. It doesn't make sense.'

Frank's mind was pounding. Martha was very perceptive, he had known that but he had had to risk her seeking answers.

He met her gaze. 'I told you he was wanting a job in order to spare you the anxiety about selling the ranch until the deal was completed. He made me an offer yesterday, I pushed the price up hoping it would be too high. It did result in him saying he would have to see what his partners said. I didn't expect them to meet my price but they did. It surprised me but it was too good to miss. If they hadn't accepted it then there was no need for you to know and you'd have been spared any worry.' Frank tried to make his story sound convincing and hoped he'd succeeded.

Martha stared at him for a few moments, wanting to believe him but was not really satisfied with the explanation.

'Oh, Frank, we've always shared everything. We've never held secrets from each other. It was not telling me, not consulting me, not letting us make this decision together which hurt.'

He leaned forward and held out his arms to her. She hesitated, met the cry for help she saw in his eyes and came to him. They held each other tight.

'I'm sorry,' whispered Frank close to her ear. 'Please approve, we'll get another place, maybe better, with the money for the ranch and what Johnny has got for the herd, I'll find a place better than the Hash Knife.'

'I don't think you could,' said Martha.

'Whatever you get won't mean the same, we built this up together.'

'It will, honey, it will,' pressed Frank.

'How much did you get?' Martha asked suddenly.

The sharpness of the question caught Frank unawares and he hadn't a ready answer. 'It's not finally settled but will be before long, the money will be paid into our bank.'

A coldness clutched at Martha's heart, a numbness gnawed at her. Frank had evaded the question. If everything had been as he had said he could have told her the price without hesitation. It would have come automatically in the pleasure of being able to name the good price he had received. Now she was even more convinced that Frank was not telling her everything. Those men must have a powerful hold over him to force him to part with the Hash Knife.

But what could she do? Frank was a stubborn man when he wanted to be and he was not a man to get angry with. Martha took a deep breath and pushed herself gently from his hold.

'All right, Frank, if this is what you've a mind to do I'll have to agree. I'll be sorry to go, I love it here so much.' The words almost choked in her throat and she had to force herself to ask: 'When do we have to leave?'

'By noon tomorrow.'

'What!' Martha taken aback by the nearness of the departure, stared incredulously at her husband. 'But I can't possibly be ready.'

'We will,' Frank tried to be reassuring, he did not want to tell his wife of Concho's threat.

Martha shrugged her shoulders in resigned despair. 'Very well.' Her feeling of dejection showed in her voice. 'What about Johnny and the rest of the men?' she asked.

'It will be up to them whether they work for Briggs or wait until we get fixed up somewhere else. We'll stay in town, I'm sure Ruth Benson will put us up until we find another place and the men return from Abilene.'

The sound of a buggy approaching the

house brought concern hurrying to Martha's face. 'The girls! What will they say?' She swung off the bed and followed by Frank hurried from the house.

The two girls were pulling the buggy to a halt in front of the veranda when their mother and father came out of the house.

'Hi, there,' the girls called as they jumped from the buggy and on to the veranda steps. Their smiles vanished when they saw the serious expressions on their parents' faces. Cathy at eighteen was the model of her mother in her younger days and because of that had a special place in Frank's heart. But that was matched equally by his affection for Clare, four years younger, for she was the tom-boy with something of himself in her.

'Something the matter?' asked Cathy glancing from her mother to her father.

'We have some news for you,' replied Martha gently, knowing that no matter how she tried to ease the announcement it would still be a shock to her daughters. 'Your father has sold the ranch.'

The two girls stared in amazement, unable to believe what they had just heard.

'But he can't!' Clare suddenly exploded. 'We like it here, we don't want to move!'

'Leave the Hash Knife!' There was a tone of incredulous bewilderment in Cathy's voice.

Martha put her arms round their shoulders and walked into the house quietly explaining what had happened.

Frank stared after them. His mind was pounding. What had he done to the wife and daughters he loved so much?

The following morning the packing, which had gone on until late into the night, was completed. Two wagons and the buggy were loaded and, an hour before noon, Frank and Martha climbed on to the wagons while Clare took the buggy and Cathy their six saddle horses.

No one looked back, no one voiced their thoughts even though everyone felt their world had been shattered. Mother and daughters, though still mystified by Frank's decision, had decided to keep silent about it and give him all the support they could.

At Ruth Benson's on the east edge of town they found a sympathetic friend who offered them accommodation until Frank could find another ranch.

At noon precisely three horsemen rode down the gentle slope towards the Hash Knife. Concho kept his horse those few inches in front of the other two, giving him the mark of authority, impressing upon Ed and Wade that he was the boss.

They rode in silence, their left hands in easy control of their horses, their right hands alert by the side of their Colts. Concho was suspicious, he had a feeling things had gone too easy. Frank had protested but had shown little sign of real resistance. That wasn't to say that Frank wouldn't hit back, he might be waiting right now with rifle ready.

'We'll move in from three sides,' said Concho, after he had voiced his cautious opinion about the situation.

Wade and Ed nodded their acknowledgement of his orders and each moved away to approach the house from different directions.

The three riders matched their pace so that they would arrive at the house at the same time. Seeing Concho leave his horse a short distance from the buildings and move forward cautiously on foot Wade and Ed did likewise. The house remained silent. Concho hesitated about fifty yards from the veranda. He drew his Colt, signalled first to Wade, approaching the rear of the house, and then to Ed, moving in towards the front. The three men suddenly darted forward in a low crouching run. They reached the house without any reaction to their presence. Concho and Ed burst through the front door as Wade kicked open the back door. They met in the hallway. Concho signalled to his side-kicks to check the rooms.

'Looks as though Frank's been sensible and gone,' commented Concho when they reported that the house was empty. 'One more precaution, Wade check the stable.'

Wade hurried from the house and was back a few minutes later to report the horses all gone and the wagons, which they had noticed the previous day, were also missing. The three men relaxed.

Concho grinned. 'Wal, we got the Hash Knife easy. Now if we play things right it can be a nice cover for our other activities.'

'Like robbing stages and banks,' laughed Ed.

'Sure, but that comes later. First we've got to establish ourselves as ranchers to give ourselves a front. There's something else I want to keep my eye on. We've got the ranch, three hundred head of cattle out on the range, the mustangs which the three Hash Knife riders will be bringing in and the cash from the herd that's been sold in Abilene.'

'That was right smart of you to work that in, Concho,' grinned Ed.

'There was more to it than the money,' replied Concho. 'I worked Frank into a position where he's broke so that I might flush him out.'

'What you getting at?' queried Wade.

'If Frank was telling the truth about not using the money we took from the stage then, because he's broke, he may just go for it, and that money's going to be mine. I'll keep an eye on him in Cameron. If he leaves town I'll follow. Might be gone some time so you two settle in at the Hash Knife and try to get a line on the stages and banks around here that are worth robbing.' Concho stretched himself in the pleasure of the way things had worked out. 'One more thing, I'll leave the document signed by Frank so that, if the foreman returns from Abilene before I'm back, you can prove the money is mine.'

# SIX

'Now don't you worry, Frank, Martha and the two girls will be all right here for as long as you want.' Ruth Benson's tone reassured Frank about the genuineness of her offer. 'You've got to look for a place and that can't be done in a hurry. Better for you to do it on your own when they've got somewhere to stay. Now come along in Frank, what are you going to do with the wagon, the buggy and the horses?'

'I'll take them to the livery stable, it will relieve you of the responsibility of having them here.'

'Fine, do it after you've settled in.'

'We're very grateful, Ruth,' said Martha, with tears in her eyes. 'You're doing us a great favour.'

'What are friends for? Besides it's you who

are doing me a favour. It gets a bit lonely since Jim got knocked down by the stage. I'm glad of the company especially when I haven't got any lodgers.'

Ruth took them inside her house and, after they had seen their rooms and had some of their belongings from the wagon, Frank drove it to the livery stable where he had made arrangements for its storage along with the buggy and horses.

Brooding over his position Frank became determined to hit back. Why should he give way to Concho? Why should he knuckle under? Now, with his family settled with Ruth, he could act without their knowledge. Eliminate Concho and his sidekicks – who would know? They would not be missed. Sure they had been seen in town but they had left and Frank figured they would have kept their plans about taking the Hash Knife a secret. Strike soon before people knew they had taken it over and all would be well. Frank saw everything in his favour and by morning his decision and plans were made.

'Just going to see if I can pick up any ideas about a place, someone in town might have an idea,' Frank announced after finishing a satisfying breakfast.

Once out of sight of the house Frank hurried to the livery stable, selected one of his horses and, while it was being saddled, checked his rifle. He rode out of Cameron by the west trail unaware that the news of his departure was being voiced in a hotel room.

'Don't look as though he's packed for a long ride,' said the small boy who held a piece of wood and a knife in his hands.

'Thanks, Billy,' said Concho Briggs, swinging from the bed on which he had been lying. 'I'll check him out from here but, if he returns, you take over just like I told you.'

Concho hurried from the hotel, got his horse from the livery stable and rode out of town in the direction indicated by Billy.

Once Frank was in sight Concho adjusted his pace so as not to arouse Frank's suspicions that he was being followed. Frank's ride swung in a wide arc round Cameron and brought him on a trail which headed for the Hash Knife. Concho was puzzled. He closed the distance between them. He must not lose contact now.

Frank rode steadily towards the ranch using the natural folds in the terrain to keep his approach unknown to the occupants. He worked his way to a small hillock from which he knew he would have a perfect view of the veranda and would be well within rifle range.

Reaching the hillock, he swung from the saddle, secured his horse and removed his rifle from its scabbard. He moved swiftly to the top of the hillock creeping the last few feet so as not to be seen by anyone who might be at the front of the house. He peered cautiously from his cover but there was no one to be seen. Frank eased himself into a comfortable position and settled down to wait.

Twenty minutes later the ranch-house door opened and Ed Farnham came out.

Frank was alert immediately and lifted his rifle to a position from which he could act swiftly. The door opened again and Wade Costain walked across the veranda to lean on the rail beside Farnham.

The blood raced through Frank. Perfect. Perfect. All he needed now was Concho to join them. He'd drop him first and if he didn't get the other two straight away he'd have them pinned down on the veranda, it would only be a matter of time.

'Come on, come on.' Frank's words were only a whisper as he willed Concho to come out. The seconds seemed eternity. His brain raced. Should he kill these two and hope to take Concho in the house? Frank started to raise his rifle to his shoulder. Then he lowered it. No, he would wait. Concho must come out some time.

'Come on, come on you bastard.' Frank was growing impatient, desiring to get the killing over.

There was a click of a gun's hammer being drawn back. Frank froze into tenseness. The noise had come from behind him!

'The bastard's here.' The voice was cold, mocking and menacing.

Frank rolled over slowly and found himself looking into the muzzle of a Colt. Beyond it was a dark, evil leer on a thin face from which eyes burned with an intense hatred. Then the expression was gone and a smile moved on thin lips.

'Didn't expect to see me, did you?' said Concho. Frank was speechless. 'Don't look so scared, Frank. Killing you would be a problem right now. Too many questions would be asked. So you're lucky.' Concho's voice suddenly went cold and menacing. 'But try this again and you'll pay and pay good through your wife and daughters!'

Frank's lips tightened. He was hooked. The position was impossible and, though his eyes spelled all the hatred he knew for the man who had come from the past to wreck his life, he could do nothing.

'Now git!' Concho stepped back and to one side keeping his gun trained on Frank who scrambled to his feet and slithered down the slope to his horse.

Concho kept his vigilance until Frank was on his way to Cameron, then he eased the hammer on his Colt and slipped the gun back into leather. He went to his horse and, after a brief visit to the house to acquaint his side-kicks with what had happened, he too returned to Cameron.

As he went into the hotel, Concho winked at the boy who was sitting on the steps whittling at a piece of wood. Both men were back in town and Billy's watch started again.

On his ride back to town Frank had puzzled over the question, how had Concho found him? He hadn't left the house, so had he been in town watching him? If so he would still be watching, making sure Frank left Cameron. Maybe now this would be the wisest thing to do. But a new spread meant money and he was broke. Concho Briggs had seen to that.

If he was to keep his past secret from

Martha he needed money desperately. He knew where there was plenty, hidden twenty years ago. Frank figured he could still find that secluded plateau high above the river near Moon Pass in Arkansas. Find that and his troubles would be over.

On reaching Cameron he rode straight to the livery stable and left instructions for a horse to be ready for him by nine the next morning.

Martha, seeing her husband approaching the house, came out to meet him as he turned through the gate.

'Any luck?' she asked.

'No,' Frank replied. 'I'll ride north tomorrow and see what I can find.'

'Nothing round here?' queried a disappointed and disturbed Martha.

Frank shook his head. 'I reckon it'll be better if we break right away. Being near the Hash Knife could hold too many memories.' He stopped and turned to his wife. He met her enquiring gaze. 'Martha, we'll find a new place, it will be like making a fresh start all over again.' Frank tried to sound enthusiastic but Martha was not to be fooled. Something more than leaving the Hash Knife still troubled her husband.

The following morning after collecting his favourite horse, chosen for its strength and power necessary for a long ride, Frank returned to the house where Martha had food and blankets ready for him. He packed his saddlebags, checked his rifle and Colt, said goodbye to his family and climbed into the saddle.

As Frank did so a small boy, sitting on the edge of the sidewalk, a hundred yards away, stopped whittling at his piece of wood. He pushed himself upright and, after one more glance to see Frank taking the north trail, turned and started along the sidewalk. His bare feet broke into a run and thrummed a path to the hotel. He burst through the door and, without so much as a glance at the clerk behind the desk, raced to the stairs.

'Hi you...' The clerk's protesting shout faded for the boy was out of sight and leaping up the stairs two at a time. The clerk shrugged his shoulders and went on tidying the desk.

The boy reached the first floor and quickly checked the door numbers until he found number six. His sharp knock was answered by a gruff 'Come in.'

He opened the door and, with a rush, burst into the room only to pull up sharp, with a startled look on his face, when he saw that the man reclining on the bed had his head raised and was squinting along the barrel of his Colt in the direction of the door.

Concho lowered his gun with a grin. 'Don't look so scared, I didn't blow your head off.' The grin vanished and was replaced by a more serious expression. 'Well?' The word held the anticipation that the boy had some news for which he had been waiting.

'Mr Peters is leaving town by the north trail,' the boy gasped breathlessly.

'Good work, Billy.' Concho Briggs' lips

gave a cold, mirthless smile of satisfaction. The bargain he had made with Billy, to watch and report Frank's movements, had paid off.

Billy went on to relate Frank's activities immediately prior to leaving.

The information excited Concho. It looked as if Frank was bent on making a long trip. Maybe he was heading for Arkansas.

Concho swung from the bed, got to his feet, fished in his pockets, found two dollars and handed them to Billy. 'Nobody's to know about this,' Concho warned before releasing the coin.

The boy nodded, hardly taking in the words as his eyes widened with surprised delight at the payment. His hand closed round the coins and he turned and ran from the room. He raced down the stairs and out of the front door leaving the clerk gasping at the speed of his departure.

Concho grinned at the boy's speedy departure then swung his gun-belt round his waist, fastened it, gathered up his belongings and hurried down the stairs. After paying the hotel clerk he lost no time in reaching the livery stable where, prompted by his urgings, the stable-boy saddled his horse quickly. As soon as it was ready Concho was in the saddle, sending the animal leaping forward into the open, almost knocking over a young woman who was hurrying to the stable. Concho ignored her, cursed and kicked his horse into a gallop for the north trail.

After his third wave to his family Frank did not look back. Though he felt dejected, they must still see him tall in the saddle.

He was riding on a trail he had hoped he would never have to travel but that bastard, Concho Briggs, had forced him on to it. Frank started. Had Concho forced him on to it deliberately so that he could follow him to the money? Well he'd take precautions, Concho was not going to get that money.

He crossed a rise and put his horse into a quick pace to a group of rocks a short distance ahead.

When he saw Frank cross the rise Concho spurred his horse forward but checked it near the top. He stood in his stirrups and was able to see Frank disappearing behind the rocks.

Concho grinned. 'Thought you might check your back trail,' he muttered and turned his horse to his left. He rode quickly and moved with the contour of the land until he was able to see Frank. Concho watched him patiently for an hour then, when Frank moved on, matched his pace on a parallel ride.

Although he had no evidence that he was being followed, Frank checked three times before he was convinced that his ideas about Concho's intentions must have been wrong. Now he rode easier in his mind but there would have been concern had he known that each check had been anticipated by Concho who now rode behind him convinced that he was on the trail of fifty thousand dollars.

## SEVEN

When Martha, her mind heavy with worry, and her two daughters watched Frank ride away no one spoke, no one moved, they just stood and stared after the man they loved. Though each saw his departure differently each felt as if it was a turning point in their lives, as if by watching him until the last possible moment they were clinging to the past, that when he crossed the rise life would never be the same.

When Frank disappeared a tension flowed from Martha and she felt exhausted. The days of pretending that nothing was wrong, that she accepted Frank's words as the whole truth, were over and now she felt drained.

'Ma, what's wrong with pa?' It was Clare who put the question for both girls.

Martha smiled wanly. 'Don't rightly

know,' she replied as they started slowly towards the house. 'He's been strange ever since those three men rode in and bought the ranch. There's something peculiar about the whole affair but I don't know what, wish I did.'

'You think there's some other reason for pa selling the ranch?' said Cathy.

'Could be, but what?'

Neither girl had an answer or even a guess but Cathy made a suggestion. 'Johnny should be back soon, maybe he'll be able to help.'

Martha stopped. She looked hard at the girls. 'Talking of Johnny reminds me, he'll ride straight to the ranch. It'll be a big shock for him when he finds we aren't there. Maybe we could meet him, it will mean keeping a look-out, probably for a few days but we've nothing else to do. We'll take the buggy each day and go beyond the hill to the north of the Hash Knife.'

The two girls, pleased to be doing something, brightened at this suggestion.

'May as well start right away,' said Cathy.

'Right. Clare and I will get some food ready and some sewing to do while we wait. You go and get the buggy.'

Cathy hurried away. She was turning into the stable when a ridden horse pounded out and would have crashed into her had she not been nimble enough to throw herself out of its way. She crashed against the door, her heart beating in fast alarm at the nearness of the accident.

'You all right, Miss Cathy?' the stable-boy called with concern as he ran to her.

'Yes, thanks, Pete,' replied Cathy staring after the disappearing horseman. 'Who was that ill-mannered lout?'

'Dunno,' replied Pete. 'Stranger to me. Had his horse here a couple of days but I haven't seen him around.'

'What's his hurry?'

'Dunno. Seemed anxious to be away. Kept at me to hurry all the time I was saddling his horse.'

'Well I won't do that, Pete, but I would like our buggy quickly.'

'Right Miss Cathy.' Pete hurried away to carry out his task.

Ten minutes later Cathy drew the buggy to a halt outside Mrs Benson's house where she found her mother and sister ready to leave.

Half way to the Hash Knife Martha turned the rattling buggy off the rutted route and headed across the grassland. She moved in a wide arc parallel with the rise to her right, before swinging away from it to climb a long, gentle slope. Once over the top she found a slight hollow from which they could see far across the undulating country to the north.

'Well, girls, I reckon this is about right.' Martha halted the buggy. 'With the Hash Knife directly behind us we should be able to spot Johnny from whatever angle he rides in.'

'Hope he isn't long,' said Clare.

'So do I, love,' returned Martha. In spite of the worry which nagged her she knew she had to put on an outward composure. 'Now let's settle ourselves. Who's going to take first turn with the binoculars?'

'I will,' offered Cathy.

Two days after Ed Farnham and Wade Costain had come to the Hash Knife, the sound of many distant hooves brought them hurrying on to the veranda.

Far in the distance they saw the dust cloud rising high above a herd of mustangs heading for the ranch. They watched with interest as the herd drew nearer and admired the skilful way in which the three horsemen handled it. Within half an hour the mustangs were corralled and the three men were riding towards the house.

Surprise at seeing two strangers showed on the faces of the Hash Knife men.

'Hi,' Wade Costain got in before the riders could question the presence of the two men on the veranda. 'Your boss sold out. Hash Knife belongs to a fella name of Concho Briggs.'

The riders exchanged surprised glances. 'Never expected this,' called one of them.

'Rather sudden,' went on Wade. 'Concho has gone off to get a few matters settled. Left us here to see to things until he gets back. Mr Peters told us you were out mustanging so we've been expecting you.'

'What's our position?' queried one rider.

'Your jobs are safe if you want to work for the new boss,' explained Ed.

'Where's Mr Peters gone?'

'Don't know. Made a quick sale and left a couple of days ago.'

'In that case we'll ride for the new owner.' The statement which came from one of the cowboys was confirmed by the other two.

'Good,' smiled Wade. 'Concho was hoping you would, especially when he was told you were good mustangers. He said if you signed on to tell you to go back for more mustangs. It's something he would like to develop alongside cattle, figures the Army will need plenty of horses and he could get a good price. Spend a couple of weeks out there.'

Wade and Ed watched them go.

'That gets them out of the way. Hope the

foreman isn't long in showing up,' commented Ed.

'Ma! Ma! Something moved, way over yonder!' Cathy pointed across the flatness. 'Just to the left of that small hill.'

Martha narrowed her eyes. She saw no sign of anything breaking the stillness. She raised the binoculars, found the hill and brought it into sharper focus. Nothing. 'Did you say left?'

'Yes, ma, yes!' This was the first excitement in the three days they had spent watching for Johnny.

Martha moved her vision slowly to the left and followed the slope of the hill to the flatness. She saw no one. But under the scrutiny of the binoculars the grassland was not as flat as it appeared to the naked eye. Martha held her gaze to the left of the hill.

'See anyone, ma?' Clare queried.

'No.'

'You've imagined, Cathy,' Clare sighed.

'No. I'm certain something moved. Keep

looking, ma.'

Martha needed no bidding to do just that. In her present state of mind she would grasp at any hope and hold on until it was definite that it did not exist.

Each second seemed eternity as mother and daughters were tense with hopeful expectancy.

'Seems you must have…' Martha suddenly cut her words off. A movement! Two riders moved out of a small hollow which had kept them from view. 'There is someone!' Martha's words came in an excited exclamation, penetrating the minds of her daughters which were beginning to slip back into the dullness of monotonous vigilance. Now they were propelled into feverish excitement.

'Who, ma who?' cried Clare.

'It must be Johnny, oh it must!' Cathy willed it to be.

'Too far off to tell yet,' replied Martha. She held the two riders in her sight. They were moving at a walking pace. The moments passed. Martha straightened, the binoculars still held to her eyes. 'It … is…' The words came slowly, still filled with uncertainty. Silence.

'Ma, is it? Is it?' Both girls called at once.

No answer. Then, 'It is! It is! That's Johnny and Cap Millet with him.' With a broad smile parting her lips and an excited light of relief dancing in her eyes, Martha thrust the binoculars at Clare. 'Come on, let's go and meet them.'

All three were on their feet quickly and when they had scrambled into the buggy Martha grabbed the reins and sent the horse down the long slope. The buggy bucked and bounced on the uneven ground but its passengers did not notice the rough ride. The man they wanted was here and they were anxious to get to him.

Johnny Hines eased his tall, lean frame in the saddle. He was keen to be on but it was hot and they had ridden far. His horse was weary and he did not want to force it any faster up the long slope, but once at the top and over the next rise it would be a different matter. Then it would be downhill all the way with his beloved Hash Knife in sight.

Foreman of the spread was more than just a job to him. He had come here after the war between the States and helped Frank Peters rebuild it. Now, he returned after a successful drive to Abilene. He had got a good price for the steers and he knew that Frank would be pleased, for the money would help Frank's plans for further expansion.

Johnny pulled gently on the reins stopping his horse. As he halted beside Johnny, Cap glanced at him, wondering why the Hash Knife foreman had stopped. Cap saw sharp eyes beating through the distance, concentrating on something ahead. Cap followed his gaze and was surprised to see a buggy coming at a fast pace down the slope.

'Where did that come from?' queried Cap.

'Don't know. I was just suddenly aware of it. Never saw it come over the top. Must have been on the slope already.'

'Whoever it is is in a mighty big hurry,' Cap commented. The two men stayed where they were watching the swaying vehicle. ‘Three women!’ Cap added in surprise.

‘Good grief, it’s Martha Peters and her two daughters!’ gasped Johnny.

‘What the hell are they doing driving like that?’

‘Come on we’ll soon find out.’ Johnny tapped his horse and urged it into a gallop.

Almost in the same instant Cap sent his horse away. The distance between the riders and the buggy shortened rapidly and within a short time Martha was hauling hard on the reins, slowing the straining horse and finally bringing it to a halt as Johnny and Cap turned their animals alongside in a swirl of dust.

‘Johnny! Johnny!’ Cathy and Clare yelled together.

Johnny and Cap saw excitement mixed with relief and gladness and touched with worry in their eyes.

‘What’s wrong?’ called Johnny. ‘What’re you doing out here driving like that?’

‘Been waiting for you,’ Martha gasped,

drawing deeply on the air to ease her lungs after the exertion of keeping her horse under control.

'Me? Why?'

'Frank's sold the Hash Knife!'

'What!' Johnny was shattered by the news. It couldn't be right. He hadn't heard correctly. Frank would never sell the Hash Knife. Johnny glanced at Cap and saw he was equally taken aback.

'It's true,' Martha went on quickly. 'But I don't like it. Frank's holding something back. I know he is, I feel it; he's never kept secrets from me before. You know what the Hash Knife meant to him; he'd never sell unless there was more to it. You've got to help. Please find out what's happening.' A pleading anxiety had come into Martha's voice and there were tears in her eyes.

'All right, Mrs Peters just take things easy, we'll do what we can.' Cap's voice was quiet, reassuring, trying to bring some calm to the rancher's wife. 'Where's Frank now?'

'He left three days ago.'

'Left?' Johnny's puzzled surprise was evident.

'To look for another ranch, a new place to live.'

'Where'd he go?'

'I don't know. Said he'd head north. But I don't like it. Frank's never been the same since the day Concho Briggs rode in.'

'Concho Briggs? Never heard of him. Have you, Cap?' Johnny turned to the weather-beaten man whose hunched appearance in the saddle belied a hidden power and determination.

Cap shook his head. 'No.' He looked at Martha. 'I think you'd better tell us all you know.'

Martha brushed the hair back from her forehead and paused a moment gathering her thoughts together. Once she started to speak she related the events, as she knew them, quickly and precisely.

'I knew you'd head for the ranch so we decided to meet you before you got there,' Martha concluded. 'Wanted you to hear the news from us rather than from strangers.' A thankful relief came into her eyes, she was pleased to have someone to share her worries. 'I'm so glad you're back, Johnny, and pleased you're here too, Cap.'

'Glad you stopped us going to the ranch,' said Johnny. 'Gives us a better chance to investigate these three men when they don't know who we are. Can you describe them?'

Martha nodded, thought for a moment then gave Johnny the information he wanted.

'That's a great help,' said Cap when Martha had completed her description. 'Now I suggest you go back to town to … er … Mrs Benson's did you say?' Martha nodded. 'Right go and stay there until we contact you.'

'We'd better not ride to town with you,' said Johnny. 'If any of these three are in town we don't want them to know there's any connection between us.'

Martha turned the buggy, called her thanks, and sent the vehicle rumbling in the direction of Cameron.

Johnny and Cap watched it until it disappeared over the rise.

'Well, the end of the drive gone sour,' commented Johnny. 'Cap, I understand if you want to ride on. There's nothing to hold you here.'

'There sure is. I wasn't foreman of the Hash Knife before the war without having some feeling for the place and for Frank and his family. There's trouble here, Johnny, so I'll stay until we solve it one way or another.'

Johnny smiled. 'Glad to have you along.'

'What now, visit the Hash Knife?' asked Cap.

'I think we'll do some checking with the sheriff first,' said Johnny. 'See if he's got anything on these fellas, and I'd like to call at the bank and deposit the note for the sale of the cattle.'

Cap agreed and the two men headed for Cameron, swinging wide in their ride so as not to approach the town from the same direction as Martha and the two girls.

There were no customers when they

entered the bank and an enquiry if the manager was available sent the clerk scurrying to another office from which he returned, a moment later to show them into a small but neatly furnished room. A stout man rose from behind an oak desk and extended his hand to Johnny.

'Glad to see you back. Hope you had a good drive and got a good price for the steers.'

'Glad to be back,' replied Johnny, shaking the man's hand firmly. 'A tricky drive at times but we won through and got a good price.'

'Splendid, splendid, Frank will be pleased.' The manager glanced at Cap and Johnny made the introductions. 'Haven't I heard of you?' added the manager thoughtfully.

'I was foreman at the Hash Knife before the war,' said Cap.

The manager nodded. 'Sit down,' he indicated the chairs and resumed his place behind his desk. 'Got a surprise when Frank sold the ranch, rather sudden, wasn't it?'

'Only just heard,' said Johnny. 'We got a shock, I can tell you. And then we learned Frank had left town.'

The manager showed mild surprise. 'Now you come to mention it I haven't seen him around though I have seen Mrs Peters and the girls.'

'He's not been in here?' asked Cap.

'No.'

'Not even to deposit cash from the sale of the ranch?'

'No. But he doesn't necessarily have to come in, the transaction might be done through credit on another bank – one through which the buyer deals.'

'Has any large sum such as that been credited to Frank's account?' asked Johnny.

The bank manager smiled. 'Client's accounts and transactions are confidential, Johnny, you know that.'

'Sure,' agreed Johnny, 'but I was hoping you might make an exception in this case.'

'Is there any reason why I should?'

'We're concerned for Frank and the

family. Selling the Hash Knife was not in keeping with Frank's thinking. It was all rather sudden, a surprise even to Mrs Peters. We're going to do some investigating, starting with the sheriff when we leave here.'

The manager looked thoughtful. 'Don't know whether that's good enough grounds to reveal confidential matter. Maybe if Mrs Peters approved…'

'She's in rather an upset state,' said Johnny. 'I don't want to cause her any more worry.'

The bank manager pursed his lips as he tried to make a decision. He looked hard at Johnny then, his mind made up he said, 'Seeing Frank's was a strange action and you're a close friend of the family, I'll make an exception. I'll take it on myself to tell you that no large sum of money has been put into Frank's account.'

Johnny and Cap exchanged meaningful glances of concern.

'Thanks,' said Johnny. 'We're grateful for your confidence. Now, can I leave this note concerning the sale of the cattle to be credited to Frank's account?' He fished in his pocket as he was talking, withdrew a piece of paper and passed it over to the bank manager who unfolded it and scrutinised it carefully.

'All in order,' he said. 'I'll see to it.'

'Thanks,' said Johnny, rising to his feet, 'and thanks again for the information.'

The two men took their leave and as they unhitched their horses from the rail outside the bank Johnny said, 'Strange that no money for the ranch has gone into Frank's account.'

'You don't think Frank's up and left altogether?'

'You mean left Martha and the girls?' Johnny was surprised by Cap's suggestion.

'Yes, funny things happen, you know.'

'Sure, but I can't see that. Frank was devoted to them.'

'Oh, I think like you, I was just exploring possibilities.'

'I reckon we're on the wrong trail there.'

The two men started to lead their horses along the street. 'Something nags me,' went on Johnny. 'I'll never believe Frank would sell the Hash Knife freely.'

'You mean he was forced?'

'It's another possibility, and if there's an answer to that then it takes in the identity of these three men. Maybe the sheriff can help.'

## EIGHT

They found the sheriff in his office but their query about Briggs and his sidekicks brought a shake of the head from the sheriff.

'Sorry, they mean nothing to me. I know they were in town, caused no trouble, then I heard Briggs had bought the Hash Knife. Mighty surprise to me but there you are, Frank's free to do as he likes.'

'So you know nothing about their past. Anything might help. Anything to connect them with Frank?'

The sheriff looked curiously at Johnny. 'Nothing. But what you getting at? Something wrong?'

'We just don't like what's happened,' replied Cap.

'Now see here, if you're holding anything

back from the law...' the sheriff let the unspoken words utter his warning.

'We'll not do that, sheriff,' reassured Johnny. 'If anything crops up that needs you we'll let you know.' Johnny turned for the door but stopped when the lawman spoke again.

'Of course if it's way back in the past, in another part of the country I'll not know.'

Johnny nodded and he and Cap left the office.

'Could be I suppose,' said Johnny, 'but where do we start?'

'Martha.'

'But we wanted to spare any more worry.'

'Sure, but if we think the past might have something to do with the situation she's probably the only one who can help. We needn't tell her that the money for the ranch is not in the bank.'

'Right. Well now that we're at this end of town we may as well book our rooms at the hotel.'

They led their horses to the next block

where they tied them to the rail outside the hotel.

'Do any jobs for you, mister?' The query came from a young boy, whittling at a piece of wood, as he sat in the shade of the sidewalk's awning outside the hotel.

'Not just now, sonny,' replied Cap as he strode by.

Johnny grinned and winked at the youngster. 'Still picking up a few bucks, Billy?'

'Yeah, but trade's a bit slack right now.'

The two men laughed and went into the hotel. The clerk glanced up from the paper he was reading and straightened when Johnny and Cap came to the desk.

'Hi, Johnny, want a room now you've no Hash Knife to go to?'

'That's the size of it, Ron,' answered Johnny. 'This here's Cap Millet, wants a room as well.'

The clerk wrote their names in his register. 'Can't say I like the look of the hombres who have bought the Hash Knife,' said Ron casually. 'Not that they gave any trouble, mind, they were quiet enough.'

'They stayed here, then?' Cap was quick to seize on the information and he shot a hopeful glance at Johnny.

'Sure. See, their names.' He ran his finger down his register and turned it for Johnny and Cap to see.

'Know anything about them?' queried Johnny.

'No. Booked in, Costain and Farnham stayed all day but Briggs rode out of town. He returned and next day all three left – booked out. But funny thing, they returned in the afternoon and booked in again. See here's their names again.'

The clerk pointed to the second entry. The two men glanced at the page but Cap's eyes travelled further down.

'I see Briggs has been back again.' Cap indicated another entry near the bottom of the page.

'Sure he came back, stayed two nights.'

'Know why?'

'No, don't pry into what my customers do.'

'Say where he was going when he left?'

'No but I presumed the Hash Knife.'

Johnny nodded. 'Thanks, Ron. We'll be back shortly for the rooms.'

'Any time.'

The two men left the hotel.

'Want any jobs doing now, mister?' Billy greeted them as they came out of the door.

Johnny grinned at him and the two men went to their horses.

'Funny thing Briggs spending two nights in the hotel after he'd got the Hash Knife,' mused Johnny.

'Did you see those dates when Briggs was in the hotel on his own?' asked Cap a note of excitement in his voice.

'No,' said Johnny.

'They correspond to the time Frank would be in town.'

Johnny stared at Cap. 'Do you think there's a connection?'

'Could be just coincidence but it could be one more strange happening to add to the other peculiarities of the affair,' replied Cap.

'Wonder what Briggs was doing in town?'

Johnny's eyes suddenly brightened. 'Maybe we can find out. Billy. He's always outside the hotel touting for jobs. He'd see Briggs come and go. Maybe he can tell us something.'

Billy looked up from his whittling when the two men came and squatted beside him. 'Thought of something?' he asked with a hopeful twinkle in his eye.

'You might be able to help us.'

'Cost you.'

The two men grinned. Cap handed the boy a dollar. 'How's that for a start?'

Billy looked quizzically at Cap. 'There's more?'

'Could be,' replied Cap. 'Depends.'

Billy was still staring at him. 'I don't know you, mister. Know Johnny.'

'Name's Cap,' he smiled and held out his hand. 'Nice to know you, Billy.'

Billy shook hands. 'Guess with a name like that you were in the war. Who'd you fight with?'

Cap glanced at Johnny who quickly put in, 'Cap fought with the North, Billy, but he's no worse for that, got to admire him for fighting for what he believes. Billy's pa was killed fighting for the South,' he explained to Cap.

Cap realised they were in a tight situation. Billy might just put up a shield of hostility and refuse to co-operate.

'I'm sorry about that,' said Cap.

Billy looked long at the stick at which he had been whittling. He was obviously deep in thought and the two men guessed it was best not to speak. They looked anxiously at each other.

Billy raised his head slowly and looked at Johnny. 'Is he really a friend of yours?'

'Sure,' replied Johnny. 'He's just helped with the Hash Knife trail drive. Used to be foreman of the Hash Knife before the war.'

The boy looked hard at Cap. 'Guess you didn't kill my pa, could have been anyone. And if you're a friend of Johnny's you must be all right.'

Both men glanced at each other with relieved smiles.

'Well, how can I help you?' asked Billy.

'Three men stayed in the hotel a short time ago,' said Johnny.

'About the time Mr Peters sold the Hash Knife,' put in Cap.

'Yes, I remember.'

'One came back to town and stayed in the hotel on his own.'

'Yes. He was a good customer of mine.'

Cap glanced at Johnny and saw that he too was wondering if they were on to something.

'What did you do for him?' asked Cap.

Billy did not answer. He looked from Cap to Johnny and then back to Cap. 'That's a bit difficult. I promised not to tell.'

'It's important we know,' pressed Johnny.

Billy looked glum. 'But I promised.'

'Sure,' agreed Johnny. 'And I wouldn't ask you to break that promise but it might be of vital importance to us and to Mr Peters.' Johnny saw Billy was weighing the situation up carefully. He paused a moment and added, 'You see, we think Mr Peters might be in trouble and we want to help him.'

Billy still looked doubtful and his young face bore an expression of serious consideration. Then he looked at Johnny. 'I know you well, Johnny,' he said. 'Cap, here, I don't know but I like what I've seen so far. This here man you're talking about, I didn't like him very much even though he paid me well, so, I figure I'll tell you.'

Johnny and Cap glanced at each other with relief.

'Thanks,' said Johnny. 'Now, what did you have to do for this fella?'

'Report any moves that Mr Peters made and let him know immediately if Mr Peters looked like leaving town.'

'I see,' said Johnny, 'now tell us everything that happened.'

Billy nodded. 'Day after Mr Peters arrived in town I had to report him leaving. Mr Briggs followed. They both returned later. The...'

'Just a minute,' interrupted Cap. 'When he wasn't following Mr Peters was Briggs in the hotel?'

'Yes.'

'He never left it?'

'No.'

'So Mr Peters wouldn't know Briggs was in town.'

'Reckon not.'

'Right, go on with your story.'

'Following day Mr Peters went to the livery stable, selected one of his horses and returned to Mrs Benson's where he was staying. From the way he packed his saddle-bags I reckoned he was going to leave town for some time. I waited till I saw him take the north trail, then I ran back here and reported to Mr Briggs.'

'What did he do?'

'He was lying on the bed checking his gun but as soon as I told him Mr Peters was leaving he paid me two dollars and left the hotel.'

'Then what?' Cap prompted Billy.

'He went to the livery stable, got his horse and left town by the same trail as Mr Peters.'

'And that's all.'

'Yes.'

Cap drew another two dollars from his pocket and handed them to Billy. 'Thanks, you've been a great help.'

Billy's eyes widened at the sight of the money. 'Another two!' he gasped. 'Gee, thanks Mister Cap, you're all right.'

Cap smiled and straightened.

Johnny tapped Billy on the shoulder. 'Thanks, pal,' he said and stood up.

The two men went to their horses.

'Why should Concho Briggs be interested in Frank after he'd got the Hash Knife?' mused Cap.

'And why should he want to know when Frank left town? Looks as if Briggs expected it, seems he came to town for that reason only, otherwise he wouldn't have stayed in his room and got Billy to watch Frank.'

'I don't like it,' said Cap. 'Concho Briggs

is worth investigating.'

'Right so let's start with the two hombres he left at the Hash Knife.'

Johnny and Cap took their horses to the livery stable and, after reassuring the stableman that it would be in order, as Johnny still regarded himself as foreman for Frank Peters, they exchanged them for two fresh mounts from those which Cathy Peters had brought in.

Once the horses were saddled they lost no time in leaving Cameron.

'How we taking this?' called Cap as they rode at a fast pace on the trail to the Hash Knife. 'Riding straight in?'

'Figure it might be an idea to scout it out first,' replied Johnny.

He guided them on an approach which would bring them to the back of the house and, with still a quarter of a mile to go, called a halt in a small hollow.

'We'll go the rest of the way on foot, horses' hooves have a way of attracting attention.' Johnny swung from the saddle.

Cap followed suit, and, after securing their horses they walked to the top of the hollow from where they surveyed the ranch buildings. Except for some horses in a corral nothing moved.

'Strangely quiet,' observed Cap, 'but I suppose that's to be expected with no Hash Knife hands around and Briggs' sidekicks probably content to wait his return.'

'We'll work to the right. Use that declining spur in the hillside. That'll take us within a hundred yards then a couple of water troughs will give us a bit more cover.'

The two men moved off and a few minutes later reached the cover of the troughs without any apparent sign of having been seen.

'Back door,' whispered Johnny. 'I'll go in first.'

Cap signalled his agreement and let Johnny reach the door before he followed.

Johnny opened the door quietly and stepped into the kitchen. He moved stealthily to the opposite door and listened. The house was quiet. He opened the door slowly, peering into a passage as the widening gap increased his field of vision. No one. He stepped into the passage and froze. A voice came from beyond a door to his right on the opposite side of the passage. His step was slow and light as he moved towards it hoping that no floorboards would squeak under his pressure. Johnny flattened himself against the wall beside the door. He glanced back to see Cap peering from the kitchen and he signalled him to wait. Voices came from the room again. More distinctive this time. Johnny eased his Colt from its holster.

'Sure wish the boys in the pen could see us now, sitting in our own ranch, they'd never believe it.' A raucous laugh followed only to be stilled by a cautious reply.

'Don't go getting too big for your shoes, Ed. Remember this is Concho's ranch not ours. And don't cross him, he can be a mean bastard. We're all right as we are, we'll get our share.'

Jail-birds! Johnny was startled. Was

Concho an ex-convict too? But why come to Frank. Had their past anything to do with him?

Johnny waited no longer. He hurled the door open and stepped into the room.

Wade Costain and Ed Farnham, startled by the unexpected intrusion, jumped from their chairs and turned to face the door in one movement. Their hands clawed at their Colts but froze on the butts, for the two men respected the menace of the Colt already trained on them in the hands of a man whom, they immediately realised, would not miss a movement if they tried to outplay him. They straightened, watching Johnny carefully.

'Who the hell are you?' Wade demanded.

'Might ask you the same,' replied Johnny coldly. 'What're you doing here? Where's Frank Peters and his family?'

Wade eyed Johnny, his reply delayed by the sound of footsteps in the passage. Cap, Colt in hand, entered the room.

'Well?' Johnny pressed.

Wade smiled. 'Guess your interest gives you away – Hash Knife men? Just returned from your trail drive?'

'What if we are?'

'There's been changes since you left.'

'So it appears. Now let's have some answers.' Johnny motioned with his gun, reminding the two men that they were still at a disadvantage under its threat.

But Wade seemed to ignore that. 'Would you be Johnny Hines, foreman of the Hash Knife?' he asked.

Johnny hesitated, wondering if it was wise to reveal his identity, but there seemed no reason to withhold it. 'Yes.'

Wade glanced at Ed and both visibly relaxed. 'Put those guns away. We've been waiting for you. Why the hell did you come sneaking in like that?'

Johnny still kept his grip on his Colt. 'The ranch appeared strangely quiet, felt something was wrong so decided to investigate. Now, let's have some talking from you.'

'Can I get a document from my pocket?'

asked Wade, eyeing Johnny's Colt.

Johnny, wondering if this was a trick, hesitated then said, 'All right, but easy, this gun's liable to go off at the slightest play by you.'

'Wouldn't tempt it,' grinned Wade as he reached into his pocket and drew a sheet of paper from it slowly. 'That'll tell you everything,' he said holding it out.

'Keep 'em covered, Cap,' said Johnny. He holstered his gun and took the piece of paper. Unfolding it he started to read. 'Peters sold out!' Johnny feigned surprise. His eyes continued down the paper.

'Sure,' Wade's smile widened.

'And the sale includes the money we got for the cattle!' Johnny was astonished at this information and a glance at Cap showed that he was equally taken aback. 'Who is this Concho Briggs?'

'Partner of ours,' said Ed. 'Offered Peters a price he couldn't refuse.'

'Where's Briggs?' asked Johnny.

'Had something to settle so left us to wait

for you. Now what about the herd money?'

'We've already deposited it in the bank,' replied Johnny.

'Damn.' Wade's face darkened with annoyance. 'I guess we'd better get into town and put that right.'

'And it'll give us a chance to check if this document is genuine. I see from the date it's only three days since Briggs took over. Quick sale was it?'

'Yes,' replied Ed.

'How come? Briggs know Peters?'

'They were...' Ed started but he never finished giving the information as Wade broke in quickly.

'Briggs offered the good price for a quick sale. Now, let's get going. Ed, get the horses. Where's yours?' he put the query to Johnny.

Johnny realised that Wade had blocked Ed and now he had got him out of the house. 'In a hollow quarter of a mile away. I'll go and get them.'

'Don't bother. We'll ride two up as far as there,' replied Wade, foiling Johnny's attempt to get at Ed again.

When the four men reached the bank they soon acquired an interview with the manager.

'Like you to cast your eye over a document,' said Johnny after he had introduced Wade and Ed.

Wade handed the paper to the manager who, after reading it looked at Johnny in surprise. 'But you've just deposited this cash in Frank's name.'

'Is the document legal?'

'Unusual to include the cash from a sale unless you know what it is but I guess when the price was agreed between Frank and Briggs they took that into consideration, each was taking a chance.'

'You'd better transfer that cash into a new account in Briggs' name,' put in Wade with a smile of satisfaction. He turned to Johnny. 'I guess that concludes our business.'

Johnny accepted the dismissal. There was nothing to be gained by argument so he and Cap left the building.

'Mighty strange to include the cash from the cattle,' commented Cap as they came on to the sidewalk.

'Sure,' agreed Johnny. 'And it means that Frank has no money so what's the use of telling Martha he was going to look for a ranch.'

'Got me beat,' said Cap. 'We've only one slender chance – the past. I'm sure Farnham was going to say something about Frank and Briggs knowing each other when Costain interrupted him.'

'And Briggs is trailing Frank. I sure don't like it,' frowned Johnny. 'I guess we should try and pick up their trail.'

'Right,' Cap agreed, 'but let's see Martha first, as we planned, see if she can tell us anything about Frank's past.'

## NINE

'You leaving?' There was concern in Martha's voice when she saw the horses tied to the white pailing fence as she hurried down the path to Johnny and Cap. She couldn't blame them if they were riding on. There was nothing to hold them here. She felt the confidence, which had returned with their arrival from Abilene, slipping away. With them around she drew a new strength and comfort, now they would be gone. 'Don't quit until Frank gets back?' she pleaded.

Johnny smiled reassuringly. 'We ain't quitting, Mrs Peters. We're going to see if we can find Frank, but first have you got any idea where he might be heading?'

'No, except that he took the north trail.'

'Can you hazard a guess?' pressed Cap.

'None,' cried Martha desperately. 'I only

wish I could.'

'Anything likely to take him back to his past, something which would make him want to return to a particular place?'

'Not that I know of,' replied Martha, after considering the question for a moment. 'Frank never talked much about his past. I know he was brought up by an aunt in his early years. Came to Texas when he was about eighteen. Got a job with Jed Wilkins, family treated him like a son. Just got the Hash Knife going when Jed was killed in a fall from a horse. Shortly after that Mrs Wilkins and her two daughters died in a fever epidemic. Frank found he'd been left the ranch so stayed on. He and I married and ... well, you know the rest. But, you know, it's funny you brought this up, Frank never used to talk about his early life. I never thought anything about it and never asked him.'

'Do you know where this aunt lived?' asked Cap.

'Benton, Arkansas.'

'Maybe Frank's gone back there to look for a place,' said Cap glancing at Johnny.

'Could have. It gives us something to go on.' Johnny turned to Mrs Peters. 'Now, please don't worry, I'm sure we'll find him.'

The two men bade Mrs Peters goodbye and left Cameron by the north trail.

'Well, we've not a lot to go on, Benton worth trying?' Cap put the question.

'Guess so. I feel the answer lies in the past and Benton is our only clue to that.'

'Looks as if this town's seen better days,' Cap commented as they rode into Benton.

'Sure does,' agreed Johnny. 'A lick of paint would help. Where we starting, sheriff?'

Cap nodded. 'But careful how we play the law.'

They tied their horses to a broken rail outside the lawman's office and entered through a door which squeaked for want of oil.

The man who lolled in his chair with his feet on the desk, glanced at them with a look which revealed his thoughts, 'Who's coming to disturb me now?'

'Sheriff?' queried Cap.

The man sighed, moved his feet off the desk, looked up casually at the two men standing in front of his desk and nodded. 'Guess I should be wearing my star.' He picked up the piece of metal from his desk and pinned it to his faded shirt. 'Guess that makes it more like. Nolan's the name, Jim Nolan.'

Cap was not impressed by what he had seen so far. 'Cap Millet, Johnny Hines.' Cap introduced them both as he looked down at the broad-shouldered, thick-necked man who had filled out through inactivity. Cap judged him to be in his sixties, a man content to let things go, with an anything-for-a-quiet-life attitude. Benton was a backwater and he was content to wallow in its quietness.

The sheriff nodded. 'What can I do for you?'

'We're trying to find a friend of ours.

Heard he'd ridden into Arkansas so we figured he might come back to the place where he grew up. Name's Frank Peters,' said Johnny.

'Peters?' A thoughtful frown furrowed the sheriff's forehead. 'Ain't heard the name.'

'Maybe before your time,' suggested Cap.

The sheriff smiled wryly. 'Hardly likely. Been sheriff for thirty years and was born and bred here.'

'Then you'd remember most folk,' said Cap.

'Sure. I have a good memory and I tell you no one of the name of Peters ever lived here. Guess you've got the wrong place.'

Cap rubbed his chin thoughtfully. 'Strange, I could have sworn Frank was raised here by an aunt.'

The sheriff glanced at Cap. 'Two kids were raised here by aunts, Wes Baker, and Sloane Wilkins. You'll have to look elsewhere.'

Wilkins! The name pounded in Johnny's mind. The name of the family Frank had come to in Texas.

'Looks like it,' agreed Cap quickly, seeing from the expression on Johnny's face that he too had made the connection. 'C'm on, Johnny.'

About to say something Johnny looked at Cap and saw the warning in his eyes. Cap turned for the door after saying, 'Thanks, sheriff. Looks as if our information about Frank Peters being here must be wrong. Sorry to have troubled you.'

Johnny nodded to the sheriff and followed Cap out of the office. As he closed the door Johnny saw the sheriff leaning back in his chair and swinging his feet on to the desk. Johnny closed the door and took two quick steps to join Cap on the edge of the side-walk.

'Cap, Frank Peters, Sloane Wilkins one and the same,' said Johnny excitedly.

'I reckon so. But why take a different name when you join your family?'

'Let's go and ask the sheriff something about Sloane Wilkins.'

'No. Fellas change their names if they get

on the wrong side of the law. If that was Frank's reason then we don't want the sheriff's suspicions roused. Let's make discreet enquiries in the saloon.'

As soon as he no longer heard the feet clattering on the sidewalk, Sheriff Nolan swung his legs off the desk and pushed himself from his chair in one flowing movement reminiscent of his early days as sheriff. Two strides took him to the window from where he watched Cap and Johnny cross the road to the saloon.

He smiled to himself. I may look an easy-going lawman, but I'm no fool. Your Frank Peters and my Sloane Wilkins are one and the same. Johnny Hines, your eyes gave that away when I mentioned Sloane's name. So, Sloane, you're back up here, wonder why? Didn't you take that money with you? Too scared to come back until now? Well, I want you, you bastard even though it all happened twenty years ago. You cost me the better job of Sheriff of Pine Bluff. Sloane Wilkins,

Frank Peters, whatever your name is you owe me and you'll pay!

The sheriff watched the two men push open the batwings and disappear into the saloon. He turned from the window, checked his Colt and then the rifle which he chose from the stand of four. He hurried outside, slipped his rifle into its leather beside his saddle, swung on to the horse and rode out of Benton.

Sheriff Jim Nolan was going to take up the hunt where he had left it twenty years before.

The saloon was quiet and Cap noticed the barman eye them up and down as they crossed the floor to the long counter. They exchanged greetings and Cap ordered two beers.

'Strangers to these parts.' The barman's words were half statement, half question.

'Yes,' replied Cap. He recognised a man who liked to chat. 'Quiet town,' he added hoping to lead the barman on.

'Sure is,' he answered. 'Nothing ever

happens here. Well, not in twenty years.'

'Twenty years?'

'That sure makes it a peaceful place,' said Johnny following up Cap's lead.

'What happened twenty years ago to make it remembered?' pressed Cap.

'Couple of wild youngsters, Concho Briggs and Sloane Wilkins, held up the stage between here and Hot Springs. Guard was killed, Briggs was caught and Wilkins got away with fifty thousand dollars.'

Excitement gripped both Johnny and Cap. They had got the lead they wanted, got the connection between Frank Peters, Sloane Wilkins and Concho Briggs. And it looked as though fifty thousand dollars was the stake being played for.

'Never get a line on Wilkins?' asked Cap.

'No. Disappeared off the face of the earth. Last seen heading over Moon Pass in the mountains north of Hot Springs. He had something likeable about him, not real bad, bit wild. It was Briggs that provided the no-good influence. Got fifteen years.'

'And since then Benton has slipped into quiet ways,' said Johnny.

'Yeah. There was a lot of upheaval for a while after, sheriff got the blame for Wilkins getting away. They'd got Briggs and the sheriff held his deputy from having a shot at Wilkins, he reckoned that with Briggs caught Wilkins would give himself up and return the money, but he never did. Hard luck on the sheriff, put paid to him getting a better job at Pine Bluff.'

'Same sheriff as you have now?' queried Johnny.

'Yeah, Jim Nolan. He's kept a grudge hate against Wilkins to this day.'

'After twenty years?' Cap showed surprise.

'Who knows, they say the criminal always returns to the scene of his crime, maybe that's what Jim's waiting for.'

'Did he try to trace Wilkins at the time?'

'Oh sure, Wilkins' folks left him behind with an aunt when they went down into Texas. Jim went there but found no trace of Sloane.'

The barman moved away to serve another customer.

'Good job we didn't go back to the sheriff,' said Johnny. 'If he'd guessed about Frank from our enquiries no telling what action he'd take and with a grudge hate going that could have meant big trouble. Do you reckon Frank's after the money from the robbery?'

'Twenty years is a mighty long time to forget about it,' commented Cap, 'but let's look at it this way; Sloane Wilkins, bit wild but not bad, only a youngster finds himself, after what is probably his first crime, holding fifty thousand dollars, his partner captured and a guard shot dead; he'd be scared stiff. He'd want rid of the money so as not to get caught with it, he daren't go back to Benton.'

'So he hides the money and high-tails it for Texas and his family,' cut in Johnny excitedly.

'Yeah, he tells them what has happened, he changes his name and they cover for him.'

'When Briggs turns up he gets Frank in a position where he has no money. Martha knows nothing about Frank's past so, in order to keep it from her, Frank needs cash to buy a new spread and where's the money – still lying hidden after a twenty year old robbery.'

'And no doubt Briggs set it up that way so he could follow Frank to the money.'

'But we still don't know where to look for Frank.'

'We've got only one point to start – Moon Pass. Sloane would get rid of the money fairly soon and the last place he was seen was Moon Pass. It's the only clue we can play.'

The two men finished their drinks and acknowledged the barman's nod as they left the bar. Once on the sidewalk they stopped a man and asked him for the direction to Hot Springs. Having obtained the information they started across the road for their horses outside the sheriff's office.

'Cap there was a third horse there,' said Johnny.

'Yeah. Sheriff's, I guess.'

'It's gone. You don't think…'

'He couldn't make any connection,' said Cap answering Johnny's unspoken question. 'Just coincidence that his horse has gone.'

Nevertheless, doubt lingered in their minds as they rode out of Benton on the way to Hot Springs.

Two more enquiries took them to a trail north of Hot Springs which rose steadily through the hill country towards the solid wall of mountains.

'We could be in luck,' said Cap, pulling his horse to a halt as they breasted a rise. He indicated a lone horseman some distance ahead across a flat expanse of land.

Johnny narrowed his eyes and studied the figure. 'That's not Frank's sit on a horse.'

'Concho Briggs?'

'Or Sheriff Nolan.'

'Let's hope you're wrong. Having Briggs tailing Frank is bad enough but if the law's slipped in as well then things could be difficult.'

They held their horses until the lone rider had disappeared over a rise, then they put them into a gallop to cover the flatness as quickly as possible. Cap drew his horse to a halt a short distance away from the top of the rise.

'I'll take a look,' he called to Johnny. Tossing the reins over, as Johnny drew alongside him, Cap swung to the ground and took his spyglass from the saddlebag.

As he held the horses under control, Johnny watched Cap go into a crouching run to the top of the rise. He stopped, peered cautiously over the top and then dropped to his stomach. From his prone position he studied the situation ahead.

The land sloped gently to a wide stream about a mile away. Beyond that the trail climbed steadily for about two miles before steepening between two mountains to cross the short joining ridge. A man stood beside the stream studying the way ahead while his horse drank.

Cap raised his spyglass and focussed it on

the man. He cursed and his lips tightened in a grim line. The Sheriff of Benton was staring fixedly towards the ridge. Cap brought the spyglass up to try to see what held the sheriff's attention. Slowly and carefully, he moved it across the landscape then suddenly brought it to a stop just below the ridge. A man on horseback held his attention. He sought an identification as the horse turned back and forth across the rising ground taking its rider nearer and nearer to the ridge. Concho or Frank or some unknown rider? He couldn't be sure. He let the spyglass take his gaze slowly down the trail which twisted and turned across the rock strewn landscape. The trail disappeared behind a huge flat-topped, out-crop of rock and Cap was about to move his spy-glass quickly to the point of the trail's reappearance when a movement emerging from behind the rock arrested his gaze. He watched carefully as horse and man appeared as they moved steadily up the trail. A follower! Concho Briggs! So that must be Frank high up on the trail. And no doubt the sheriff had seen them both.

Cap slid backwards away from the edge of the rise then turned and pushed himself into a crouching run back to Johnny who was anxiously awaiting his return. Cap quickly told him what he had seen.

'Any chance of outriding the sheriff and Concho and getting to Frank first?' Johnny asked.

'No,' replied Cap. 'We'll just have to follow and hope for something better on the other side of the ridge.'

'We're going to have to wait for Nolan to cross that ridge otherwise he might see us.'

'True,' replied Cap, 'but there is sufficient cover to enable us to make some progress towards the ridge. I'll go back. Bring the horses when I signal.'

Cap hurried back up the slope, watched the situation carefully for five minutes then signalled to Johnny to bring the horses.

Johnny crossed the top of the rise quickly and stopped a few yards down the slope so that they were not breaking the sky-line while Cap mounted.

They lost no time in reaching the stream where they allowed their mounts to drink the cool, clear water while they studied the situation.

'Guess Frank must have crossed the ridge,' said Cap when he saw only the second rider high on the slope.

'Where's the sheriff?' asked Johnny. 'Guess he must be hidden by that huge outcrop of rock. It'll give us protection from him so let's go.'

They sent their horses away quickly, keeping alert to the changing situation, prepared to halt or take cover at the first sign that it was not wise to keep moving. Progress was slow. The two men were impatient, wanting to be on, fearing a confrontation between Concho and Frank before they were able to intervene, but needing to avoid discovery by the sheriff.

Once Briggs had crossed the ridge the lawman quickened his pace, forcing his mount upwards, frightened to lose contact with the man in front. Seeing this, some of the anxious tension went out of Cap and Johnny and was replaced by an urge to move as quickly to the ridge as possible. Using every available cover, they closed some of the distance between the lawman and themselves. Then he was over, out of sight and Johnny and Cap, relieved of the necessity to seek cover, made rapid progress up the slope. Their horses responded to their urgings and both animals and men were breathing heavily when they carefully crossed the ridge.

A long narrow pass was overshadowed by the precipitous walls of mountain rock on either side. The gloom they cast seemed to be hastening the night.

'See him?' whispered Johnny.

'Half way along,' replied Cap quickly.

'Hanged if I can,' said Johnny. 'Come on, we'd better keep in touch.' He tapped his horse forward. 'Hope he can see Briggs and that Briggs can see Frank or we're lost.'

'The problem's going to be getting to

Frank before it's too late.'

This laid heavily on their minds as they concentrated on keeping Sheriff Jim Nolan in view.

As Nolan moved steadily through Moon Pass he savoured in his mind the pleasure of revenge after twenty years. He had nearly thrown it, back there, on the trail when he had first sighted Sloane Wilkins. Seeing a second rider had held him back. Concho Briggs, and he was shadowing Wilkins! It could only mean one thing, the rumours that Wilkins had hidden the money which he had never believed, must be right. So the sheriff waited and followed, a new strategy worked out in his mind.

As the sharp precipitous heights gradually eased towards the end of the pass, Frank moved further to the right and concentrated on finding a track recalled from his days in Benton. He slowed his horse to a walking pace, stopping it now and again to scrutinise the ground more thoroughly. Just as he was beginning to despair he spotted what he was looking for. He rode forward, certain that before long he would have the money which would stake the future and help him forget the past once again.

The track swung round a spur above the trail where it left Moon Pass and moved out of the hills on to a broad valley. The track hugged the hillside then moved into a cleft which split the spur in two. Frank hurried his horse through the cleft and came out on to a small plateau of rock which ended in a sudden drop of thirty feet to a deep river sent rushing quickly by the narrowness of its bed at this point, to a plunging, foaming waterfall.

Frank comforted his horse against the noise of the roaring water as he rode across the rock towards its edge, a short distance up stream of the fall. He stopped his mount and slid from the saddle. As he walked towards the edge of the rock he found the years had slipped away and the serious anxiety which had gripped him twenty years ago was back. It was as if he was hiding the money not seeking it.

Reaching the edge of the plateau he dropped to his stomach and peered over. He wriggled a few inches to his right, peered over again and then reached below the edge with his right hand. He groped at the rock face, feeling for the slit and hollow in the hardness. It was solid. A few inches more. Then his hand met no resistance. Excitement seized him. He shuffled forward to get a longer reach. Below him water swirled in its foaming rush towards the fall which churned the water into a roaring, pounding mass. His fingers stretched in feeling search. They found something softer than the rock but still with a firmness. The nervous tension heightened. His fingers took a firmer grip. He eased the object gently. It resisted with the adhesion of twenty years.

Easy. Gently. Frank forced himself not to rush. One slip, one moment of carelessness and the money which would hide the past from his family would be his. He eased himself forward. From his precarious position he compelled himself to ignore the rushing water below and closed his ears to the pounding roar. He felt again. That extra inch gave him a better grip. He explored the object, now identifiable as a small sack, easing it away from the rock. Gently and carefully he got his fingers underneath, recognised the rottenness of the sack and hoped it would not disintegrate as he raised it.

His movement was slow, testing yet firming his grip all the time. He dug hard at the rock with his toes and legs as he started to take more weight with his hand. He eased the old sack off the ledge and brought it slowly into the open. He could see it! His mind raced. A fortune. His troubles over. He must not drop it now. He inched back slowly from the edge until, with only a slight turn, he was able to deposit the sack on the solid rock beside him.

He had done it! Now for the other one! He

repeated his performance with the dexterity of one who has learned from experience. As he brought the second sack back towards the security of the ground beside him he twisted round with relief at a difficult task completed successfully. But his triumphant joy was short lived, halted as it burst upon him. His eyes widened in horror when he saw himself staring into the cold muzzle of a Colt pointing straight at his head!

'Thanks, Sloane.' Concho's mocking tone was accompanied by a grin of derision.

'You bastard!' hissed Frank.

# TEN

Anger seethed in Frank. Anger at himself for being outwitted by Concho. Anger at Concho for returning from the past and out-smarting him at every turn.

'You set this up hoping I'd lead you here.' The words spat from Frank's tightly drawn lips.

Concho laughed. 'When you wouldn't cut me in I had to play it as if you were telling the truth about not using the cash from the stage.'

'Why couldn't you be content with the Hash Knife?' hissed Frank.

'Always welcome a bit more,' grinned Concho. 'And I served a prison sentence, remember? I figure you owe me interest on those years, this'll do nicely.' His eyes narrowed. Now was the moment. No point in hanging around here any longer. His finger pressure on the trigger started to increase.

Jim Nolan reined his horse to a halt at the end of the cleft. A riderless horse, its reins held by a large stone stood quietly to the right. It shuffled nervously at the arrival of a newcomer. Nolan's eyes were quickly taking in the scene across the small rock plateau.

Briggs was standing over a figure prone on the ground, who was reaching over the edge of the rock. The sheriff figured that Wilkins was recovering the money for something lay beside him. Briggs half turned and Nolan saw he had a Colt pointing at Wilkins. An urgency almost bordering a panic seized him. He slipped quietly from the saddle dragged his rifle from its scabbard and hurried to the cover of a boulder a few yards on to the plateau. He didn't want Wilkins killing. Concho didn't matter, he served time but Wilkins was different, he had to pay, pay for all the years he, the sheriff, had been forced to stay in Benton. Wilkins had to be taken alive, death was too swift, he had to know he was paying for a twenty year old crime.

The sheriff saw Wilkins retrieve the second sack and freeze as he turned over and saw Briggs. Nolan raised his rifle, steadied it on the boulder and carefully aimed at his target – Concho Briggs.

There was a crash and the sound of the shot reverberated on the rock until it was overwhelmed by the noise of the river.

Frank stared wide-eyed as the man towering over him jerked and staggered.

There was another loud roar but much closer this time. Frank recoiled under its impact and jerked as the bullet from Concho's Colt split the rock close to his head.

Concho's eyes widened in disbelief at the pain which seared through his body. His legs began to buckle. Unable to understand what had happened his instinct was still directed to killing Frank. He tried to level his Colt again. Frank saw the movement and kicked out desperately. His feet caught Concho just below the knees. Concho staggered sideways as his legs gave way. He lost his balance and made one desperate effort to regain it as he stumbled off the edge of the plateau. His piercing scream rose above the pounding water and then was suddenly cut short as the water closed over him.

Frank scrambled quickly to his feet and from the rock's edge stared down into the tumbling, foaming water. The whiteness danced and boiled in seeming joy at having claimed a victim. Frank's gaze moved towards the falls. He stiffened. An object, foreign to the roaring water was churned to the surface. It tumbled over and over. Concho! There was no effort from him, no battle to stop his helpless rush towards the plunge. Then he was gone in a sweep of water pounding its way into foaming depths.

'Wilkins! Sloane Wilkins!'

The words came, hardly distinguishable, to Frank's ears. He froze into startled fright. Concho called his name! He stared unseeingly at the water swirling below. But he had seen Concho go over the falls.

'Wilkins!'

There it was again. Louder, because this time it penetrated his numbed brain.

'Wilkins!'

The voice was behind him. Distinct.

Frank spun round. He stared across the plateau. A man, his head and shoulders showing above a large boulder, shouted his name again. This was no ghost. This was not Concho. But who else knew his name? Who else knew he was here? Frank's brain was awhirl with puzzling questions. Concho's side-kicks? But there was only one man. There was a movement and Frank saw the rifle. So this was the man who had shot Concho. This was the man who had saved his life. A certain measure of relief surged in Frank. He had this man to thank. He relaxed a little. But who knew his real name?

'Wilkins! Unfasten your gun belt!'

Suddenly Frank was tense again. Wary, suspicious. He hesitated.

'Get on with it!' Now there was anger in

the voice. 'I don't want to kill you yet, but I will if I have to, so just do as you're told.'

Puzzled and bewildered, saved from certain death only to be threatened again, Frank slowly unbuckled his gun belt and let it drop at his feet.

'Twenty years is a long time to wait, Wilkins, but you turned up as I always figured you would.'

'Hold it!' cut in Frank sharply. 'Who are you?'

A harsh laugh rang across the plateau. 'Sheriff Jim Nolan! Remember me?'

Frank gasped. The law! How had the law caught up with him after all this time and here at the place where he had hidden the money? 'Sure, I remember you.' Frank forced his voice to sound calm.

'Well, now you're going to pay. I got the blame for letting you escape. Lost the chance of becoming Sheriff of Pine Bluff through that. I've waited twenty years for my chance of revenge and now I'm going to take it.' The sheriff's voice rose, relishing in the delight he was going to extract in his method of revenge.

Frank's mind raced. He sensed the sadistic streak in the sheriff and knew that one swift, sure shot was not going to extinguish his life. He was going to be made to suffer and Nolan was going to take delight in it. He glanced round, desperately seeking some means of escape.

'Forget it,' laughed Nolan. 'There's no cover. I'd drop you before you got two yards.' His voice changed suddenly. Now there was a snarling viciousness about it, demanding instant obedience. 'Kick your gun belt into the river.' Frank did as he was told. 'Now, move towards me. Just don't want you falling over the edge like Concho.'

Frank moved slowly.

'Stop, right there!' yelled Nolan, after Frank had walked eight paces. 'Now I'm going to tell you what I'm going to do just so you can enjoy it! I'm going to put a bullet in each leg and each arm and then I'm going to leave you to rot in this place.'

Frank stiffened with the horror of the sheriff's idea. His nerves were taut. 'Thought you'd be taking me in, you being a lawman,' he called.

Nolan laughed. 'Might have done one day, but I've had time to nurse my hatred of you. Taking you in would be too good for you. Oh, I know you'd serve your time but you'd get out one day and still be a threat to me.'

'Threat?'

'Sure, 'cos I'm taking that money!'

Frank was startled. So the sheriff was playing for big stakes! No one would know because no one ever came to this spot and if and when they did they'd find only his heap of rotting bones with no indication as to who he was or why he was there.

'That surprise you, Wilkins? Nothing to say? You owe me and the law owes me so I'm heading out with that cash.' He paused a moment. 'You ready, Wilkins?' He raised his rifle slowly and took careful aim at Frank's right knee.

Johnny and Cap were a quarter of the way into the cleft when they heard two shots. They cast a startled look at each other.

'Rifle,' said Cap, 'and then a Colt.'

Johnny pushed his horse quickly without comment. He was anxious for Frank and he hoped they were not too late. Two shots, different weapons was ominous. Two shots and three men ahead of them.

Nearing the end of the cleft the two men halted their horses and were out of the saddles almost before they had stopped. They ran forward quickly, drawing their Colts as they did so. Using every available cover they were soon positioned behind a huge boulder at the end of the cleft about five yards behind Sheriff Nolan. Peering cautiously round their cover they took in the scene. As the sheriff taunted Frank with his plans, Cap indicated to Johnny by signs what he was going to do. Johnny nodded his agreement and motioned to Cap that he would be ready as a back-up should anything go wrong.

Cap braced himself. The situation was becoming explosive. He needed to cross five yards of open without discovery. He eased himself round the boulder and steadily moved towards the lawman.

'You ready Wilkins?' The sheriff's voice boomed.

Johnny stepped quietly from behind the boulder and stood in the open with his Colt levelled at the sheriff ready to blast him if Cap did not reach him in time.

The sheriff's rifle came to his shoulder. He squinted down the sights, his aim methodical and deliberate.

Cap launched himself. He pounded against the unsuspecting lawman whose rifle fired harmlessly into the air as he crashed against the boulder. Before the sheriff could catch a glimpse of his assailant, Cap brought the barrel of his Colt across the back of the head. Nolan's mind exploded into unconsciousness and, as Cap straightened taking his weight off him, he slid to the ground.

It was all over in a moment but already

Johnny was holstering his Colt as he ran towards Frank.

Frank stared in amazement, hardly able to believe what he saw. Everything had happened so fast that it didn't seem possible that he had been pulled back twice from the brink of death in so short a time. But who were his rescuers? Or were they going to be like the sheriff, merely after the cash. Frank's mind was beginning to race when it stopped with a jolt. Johnny! It couldn't be! Yet it was! Johnny Hines was running towards him. Then the man, whom he had seen only as someone crash into Nolan at the final moment of the attack, appeared from behind the boulder. Cap! Cap Millett! Frank stared incredulously at the two men.

In a few moments they were hugging each other in pleasure and Frank was pouring out his thanks and assailing their ears with questions.

When some sort of calmness returned to the three of them, Johnny put the question to Frank. 'Where's Concho Briggs?'

Frank told them quickly about the shooting and Concho's fall into the river. As he did so he realised that his past was no longer his secret. 'You know about twenty years ago?' He put the question but already knew the answer.

The two men nodded. 'We've pieced things together,' explained Cap, 'and I figure we were about right. It was confirmed when we heard Sheriff Nolan calling you Sloane Wilkins.'

The dejection which filled Frank showed on his face. He glanced from one man to the other. He saw sympathy in their eyes.

'I hope you're going to keep this to yourselves.' He spoke quickly, almost anxiously. 'I should hate Martha to know.'

Cap glanced at Johnny. 'Sure,' they agreed, but both wondered how long Frank could go on hiding his secret.

'Good,' said Frank. The measure of relief in his voice was noticeable. 'Then let's hit the trail for Cameron and the Hash Knife and get Concho's two side-kicks out of there.'

'That may not be so easy,' said Cap. 'You signed a document handing over the Hash Knife and the money from the cattle drive, to Briggs. Fight it and Martha will have to know the truth.'

The realisation that Cap was right struck Frank forcibly. 'Then I'll forget it, take this money and start elsewhere just as I was going to.'

'You're not going to hand the money back?' Johnny stared incredulously at his boss. Was there still something of the wild young Frank left?

'If I do that I'm broke. Martha thinks I sold the Hash Knife and that there's money from the drive, this money has got to provide that cover.'

'Don't be a fool,' Caps words were sharp. 'Keep that cash and you're putting yourself further outside the law.'

'But Martha and the girls...' started Frank.

'Trust them,' cut in Cap roughly. 'Tell them. If I know them it won't alter their feelings for you. The Frank that robbed that coach is not the Frank they know. You haven't changed to us because we know about your past. Isn't that so, Johnny?' he turned to the Hash Knife foreman for support.

'Sure is,' replied Johnny quickly. 'What you did twenty years ago bears no resemblance to the man I know, a good, honest, hard-working boss, considerate to his men and family. And that's the man I still work for.'

Frank's lips tightened. His mind was awhirl with all the possibilities as he tried to weigh up one course of action with the other. Twenty years of a good life, of happiness couldn't be wiped out just like that with the admission of his guilt. Martha was strong enough to rise above it, he really knew that but he had always nursed a little doubt, until his early life had faded so far in the past that he had almost forgotten about it and there became no need to tell Martha. Now, recent events had brought the past pounding into the present with a viciousness which had renewed the fears of his courting days and early marriage and had scared him into panic action to keep the knowledge from Martha.

'...besides if you keep that money do you think Nolan's going to rest?' Cap's words began to penetrate Frank's thoughts. 'After what we heard he'll come hunting for you just for the cash. Hand it over to the authorities and Nolan's objective is gone. I don't think he'd hunt you for revenge only, besides if he found Frank Peters in Cameron who there would believe his story that Frank Peters was Sloane Wilkins, stagecoach robber?'

'I guess you're right,' Frank said with a shrug of his shoulders. 'But when I take that money in I'm going to be arrested.'

'You won't take it in. We will,' said Cap. 'So no one will know that Sloane Wilkins has been back after twenty years.'

'Only the sheriff,' added Johnny, 'and he ain't going to say anything or he'll be admitting to letting Sloane Wilkins slip through his fingers again.'

Frank saw that his friends were right. He gathered up the money and handed it over to Cap.

'It sure would have come in useful,' he said with a wry grin.

'We'll figure a way of dealing with Concho's side-kicks and getting the Hash Knife back.' Cap's words were reassuring.

## ELEVEN

The three men left the unconscious form of the sheriff beside the boulder, recovered their horses and rode through the cleft to Moon Pass where they turned in the direction of Hot Springs. Once clear of the pass they cut across country to Benton.

Three miles out of the town they split, with Frank making for a pre-arranged meeting place south of the town and Cap and Johnny riding towards the main street.

The town was quiet as the two men swung from their saddles in front of the bank. Taking one sack each they entered the building and asked for the bank manager. The only clerk hurried away and a few moments later a door opened and a man in his sixties, neatly dressed, looked frankly at them as he asked them to come into his office.

'Well, gentlemen, what can I do for you?' he asked as he closed the door.

'We have a large deposit to make,' said Cap.

'Certainly, how much?'

'Fifty thousand dollars!'

'Fifty thousand dollars!' the bank manager gasped.

'Right. We want it depositing in the bank's account and a receipt for it.'

'The bank's account?' the manager was puzzled.

'It belongs to the bank. We found it in the hills and it recalled a stage robbery of twenty years ago that we heard some talk about when we came up here a few days ago.'

Cap and Johnny dumped the two sacks on the desk and the bank manager flopped into his chair staring at the sacks in wide-eyed amazement. He couldn't believe it after all those years.

'Sheriff wasn't in so we came here,' said Johnny to bring the manager back to reality.

The manager looked up. 'Quite right, quite right,' he said quickly. He pushed himself to his feet, opened the door which led to the area behind the counter and called to the clerk to lock the outside door and then to come into the office.

'Help me check this,' said the manager when the clerk came in.

The clerk stared in amazement at the heap of money when the manager emptied the sacks. The two men started counting.

'Not a dollar missing.' The bank manager straightened and eased his back. 'Well, I can tell you I've never heard of the money from a robbery being recovered after twenty years. Wish the dollars could talk and tell us what happened.'

'Good job it can't,' thought Johnny.

'Well, gentlemen, the receipt.' The manager selected a sheet of paper and started to write. 'Your names?' he glanced up.

'Cap Millett and Johnny Hines.'

'Where from?'

'Doesn't matter,' replied Cap.

The manager hesitated then said, 'Suppose not.' He completed the receipt, straightened and handed it over with a smile. 'And now, you're a thousand dollars richer.'

'What!' both men gasped at once.

'There was a thousand dollars reward at the time for recovery of the money. I guess it still stands and you're entitled to it.'

A few minutes later Cap and Johnny were riding out of Benton with the money in their saddle bags.

After meeting Frank they put their horses into a quick pace to put as much distance between Benton and themselves before making camp for the night.

Once they had settled down Cap and Johnny, as pre-arranged, took the packages from their bags and handed them over to Frank.

'What's this?' he asked.

'The reward.'

'Reward?'

'For the recovery of the money.'

Frank stared from one to the other. 'After

all this time?'

'Bank manager said so.'

'It's not mine, it's yours.'

'You recovered the money.'

'Yes but I wouldn't have had it if you hadn't arrived. To save any more arguments we'll split it three ways.'

Johnny and Cap, knowing it would be useless to argue, accepted Frank's decision.

Frank started to count out the money, then he stopped and burst out laughing. 'Guess I'll be the only stagecoach robber in history to get a reward for the money he stole!'

It was mid-morning when the three men saw Cameron. Glad to be back, eager to see Martha and the girls, Frank pushed his horse into a quicker pace. Johnny and Cap matched it and they approached Ruth Benson's without going through town.

As they swung from the saddles, Ruth came hurrying from the house.

Frank smiled, pushed open the gate and

held out his arms. 'Ruth! How nice to see you. It's great to be back. Where's Martha and...' His words faded and his arms dropped when he saw the serious expression on Ruth's face. There was no warmth, no welcome in the eyes, only concern and worry tempered a little by the relief at seeing him. Something was wrong! The smile vanished from Frank's face for he felt whatever it was concerned Martha.

'Oh, Frank, I'm so glad you're back!' The tone of Ruth's voice brought Johnny and Cap turning from their horses. All was not well.

'Martha, where's Martha?' asked Frank with concern.

'Two days ago two men came, asked her and the girls to go with them, said it concerned you. They've not been back.'

'What!' Frank was stunned. 'Who would want Martha and the girls? Why?' Alarm blurred his mind from clear thinking.'

Then Cap and Johnny were beside him. 'Mrs Benson, what were the men like?'

There were tears of worry and concern in Ruth's eyes as she looked at Johnny. 'I've never seen them before. One was stocky, the other taller. I didn't like the look of them but the tall one gave me the shivers, mean mouth and cold grey eyes which seemed to bore right into you.'

Each of the men then knew the answer. It was Frank who spoke their names with a venomous hatred which bore them no good. 'Costain and Farnham.' He swung on his heels and strode to the gate.

Cap, who had recognised a rage which would blind Frank to caution, hurried after him. He must calm that rage to save Frank from doing anything foolish.

'Thanks, Mrs Benson,' Johnny stayed a moment to offer comforting words to Ruth. 'We know these men; we'll see that Mrs Peters and her daughters are safe. Go inside and try not to worry; we'll take care of everything.'

Johnny turned and hurried to his horse. Frank and Cap were already in their saddles and sending their mounts in the direction of the Hash Knife. Johnny unfastened the reins, placed his left foot in the stirrup and swung upwards as he touched the horse. The animal was into full gallop before Johnny had settled in the saddle. He urged it faster and slowly closed the gap to Frank and Cap.

Earth flew beneath the flaying hooves beating out a rhythm which pounded questions into Frank's mind. Why had Costain and Farnham kidnapped his family? Had they taken them as a precaution against his return? But why? They must have known that Concho had gone after him and therefore would not expect him to return. Had they heard of Concho's end? But how? The answers would not come and gradually the thundering hooves hammered them from his mind leaving only the call of rescue pounding in his brain.

He was oblivious of the men riding beside him and to Johnny who had all but overtaken them.

Cap had yelled more than once at Frank

but the ranch owner had not heard or paid no heed. He saw the angry set of Frank's jaw and knew that unless he called a stop, Frank would go riding blindly into the Hash Knife which would be fatal to everyone.

They were riding fast up the slope which gave on to the rise of land a mile from the ranch-house when Cap moved his mount nearer Frank.

'Ease up, Frank, ease up! You can't ride straight in!' he yelled.

The words were torn away by the wind and Frank took no notice.

Cap shouted again bringing a startled look to Frank's face. Cap pressed home his advantage. 'Haul in! You ride straight in they'll likely kill Martha.'

These final words seemed to pierce Frank's mind. Kill Martha! He hauled on the reins gradually slowing his horse and finally pulling it to a dirt-stirring halt.

A measure of relief spread over Cap and he brought his horse to a sliding stop. Johnny reined hard thankful that the headlong rush was being halted. Now they might have a chance of sizing up the situation in a calmer frame of mind. The horses milled as their riders settled them. Heaving bodies of both animals and men, gulped at the air, drawing deep breaths into their tortured lungs.

'Calm it, Frank.' Cap was the first to speak. 'We mustn't endanger Martha or the girls. Let's move cautiously and see what those two bastards want.'

Frank nodded. 'You're right. I was blinded by everything but getting to Martha. Thanks.'

'Right,' said Cap. 'Can you think of any reason why they should take Martha?'

Frank shook his head. 'None. They must want a hold over me, but what for, I don't know.'

'They'd expect Concho coming back, not you,' said Johnny, 'so it can't be against your return.'

'All right,' said Cap, 'it doesn't really matter, we'll have to play things as they come in any case. I figure we should split as a precaution. Johnny how long before you can be round the far side of the house?'

'Give me fifteen minutes. I can make it a fast ride keeping below the skyline with this rise swinging round the house.'

'Good. We'll give you that time, then we'll ride slowly in and see if we can make any sense out of this. Get as close as you can by the time we reach the house and play it from there taking your cue from us.'

Johnny nodded, turned his horse and rode off.

Wanting to be on, the next fifteen minutes seemed to drag to Frank. Cap saw his anxious eagerness and did all he could to keep him calm. An over-wrought, over-anxious man could be dynamite in a tense situation. Things could go wrong, sparked off by some small incident or indiscretion, powered into being by a mind from which cool thinking had been driven by tense anxiety. Above all else this situation needed calmness. There were lives at stake.

# TWELVE

'Let's go!' Cap had had to resist Frank's eagerness several times. 'We must give Johnny time,' he had insisted but now he figured they should ride. 'Keep it to a walking pace.'

They crossed the rise together. Their eyes took in the scene. It was calm and peaceful, nothing to indicate that anything was wrong. Frank had seen it hundreds of times like this. It meant home, tranquillity and his loved ones. But, today, although the scene looked the same, Frank felt as if a menacing shadow was cast over it. Danger lurked down there. He was not worried for himself but for Martha, for Cathy and Clare. They must not be harmed. Thinking of them brought tenseness creeping into his body but his brain went ice-cold and crystal clear in its thinking as he swore vengeance on anyone who harmed them.

Cap rode quietly beside him. His eyes were searching the area for movement but there was none. Not even from Johnny. Cap hoped Johnny was all right, he hoped their timing had been correct. Johnny might be vital to their safety. He turned his attention back to the house. Still there was no movement. The place could be deserted for all the signs of occupation there were, but Cap felt otherwise. Eyes must be watching them now.

Johnny rode hard swinging in a huge arc, following the skyline of the rise. Judging his position, he slowed his horse, turned it towards the top of the rise until, by standing in the stirrups, he could see over the top. One glance was sufficient. He lowered himself into the saddle, turned the horse back down the slope continuing along the rise at a gallop.

The next time he stopped he was confident of his position in relation to the ranch-house.

He slid from the saddle, ran up the rise, pausing near the top to drop to his stomach and crawl the last remaining yards. He peered cautiously over the ridge. All was still before him. No sign of life came from any of the buildings. His gaze moved beyond the buildings to the far distant rise and saw two figures just starting off down the slope towards the ranch-house. He was surprised. He must have been quicker than his estimation or Frank and Cap had held off longer. No matter, it gave him more time to weigh up the situation.

The stables, lying between the rise and the ranch-house, could offer him cover and protection. He would be closer to things once he reached there. But whatever he did he must not be seen for he knew that Cap was relying on him to provide the element of surprise should things go wrong and a rescue became necessary. An open space of about a hundred yards between the stable and the house would prove the most difficult. He would have to wait until the attention of the occupants, he supposed were in the house, was fully directed at Frank and Cap and that would be difficult to judge when he could not see them.

With these problems in mind, Johnny slid over the ridge on his stomach, kept in that position for a few yards down the slope. When he knew he would not break the skyline he rose into a crouching run towards the stables, hoping that no one would come to a window at the back of the house.

There was no reaction to his movement and he was thankful for that when he reached the cover of the stable wall. He flattened himself against the wood, breathing deeply to ease his heaving lungs. Once they had been appeased he moved stealthily to a small door. He reached for the sneck and raised it slowly. He wanted no sound at this point. Gently he eased the door until a slight opening enabled him to listen to the noises inside the stable. He heard only the sound of horses breathing and champing at the hay. He pushed the door wider and looked in. Fortunately the two main doors had been left open and light streamed in revealing nothing but horses.

Johnny stepped inside and was quickly to the ladder leading to the loft. He crossed the soft hay, which was strewn on the floor, to the doorway overlooking the space between the stable and the house and was delighted to find that a cart, half filled with hay, stood below him. He had a quick get out when the time came, when every second might count. He settled himself to wait, watching the door and windows at the back of the house.

Five minutes passed then a noise alerted his attention. The back door opened and Ed Farnham came out. Johnny tensed himself when he saw him walk towards the stable. The last thing he wanted was a confrontation with anyone now. However he might remain undiscovered in the loft.

Ed Farnham was half way to the stable when Wade Costain suddenly appeared at the back door. 'Ed!' he shouted. 'Get back in there, Peters is coming!'

Ed spun round and ran for the house. He hurried straight in neglecting to close the door behind him.

Johnny found himself tense and decided to seize on the chance offered by Farnham. A quick glance across the rear of the ranch-house told him all was clear. He dropped from the opening, landing in the softness of the hay in the cart. He rolled over, swung off the edge of the cart to the ground and ran quickly to the back door of the house.

He flattened himself against the wall beside the door and listened. Voices came from the far reaches of the house but he could not make out the words. Johnny guessed the two men must be watching Frank and Cap. He drew his Colt and stepped inside the kitchen. The door leading from the kitchen into the house was closed. Ed Farnham hadn't been obliging this time. Johnny cursed his luck. He crossed to the door and listened. All was quiet. He waited. No sound. What was happening?

His curiosity overcame his caution. His

hand closed on the door knob. He was about to turn it when he heard a door open and footsteps start along the corridor. Johnny stepped to one side of the door, his Colt held up in readiness to take the unknown person should he come into the kitchen. Tension gripped him.

The footsteps came nearer and then they were past the door. Johnny relaxed, moved quickly back to the door and, hoping that it would not squeak, turned the knob and pushed the door open sufficiently for him to see along the corridor. Ed Farnham was hurrying to the stairs.

Johnny waited with the door held open the merest fraction, unnoticeable in the gloom of the corridor unless anyone was particularly observant. And when he came back Ed Farnham was not that, for his attention was otherwise occupied. Johnny stiffened when he saw Martha, Cathy and Clare escorted by Farnham pass the kitchen. He heard a door open further along the corridor then close a few moments later. He was thankful to know where the captives were. He was near, handy if needed.

He heard the door open again. Once more he prepared to receive a visitor, but once more the footsteps went past and Johnny saw Ed Farnham, rifle in hand, go up the stairs. A rifle! Johnny's thoughts raced. A precaution, ready to cut down the two riders should anything go wrong. Ed Farnham upstairs. That must leave Wade Costain alone in the room with the captives. Could he take him without harm coming to Martha and the girls? Johnny was hesitant. Even if he did the commotion could alarm Farnham who could pick off Frank and Cap from the upstairs window. Johnny decided he must wait to take Wade Costain but maybe he could take Ed Farnham out of the action.

He started to open the door wider, then stopped. A voice came from the room along the corridor. Costain, reckoned Johnny. Then he was startled when another voice spoke. Another man! So they weren't just taking on Farnham and Costain. There was someone else. Or were there more? Johnny decided he must deal with Ed Farnham and so relieve Frank and Cap from one threat. He opened the door and slipped quietly into the corridor. His stealthy movements took him to the stairs. He was halfway up when a shout froze him into immobility.

'Hold it!'

For one brief moment Johnny thought he had been seen but then that was gone when he missed the sharp clarity to the call and realised that it came from the room along the corridor and must be directed at the two riders approaching the house.

'Wilkins, leave the fella there and come on in alone.'

'Staying right here 'till I know my wife and daughters are safe.'

'They are.'

'Release them and I'll come.'

The request was answered by a sharp laugh. 'Not likely. You come and we'll let them go.'

'If that's you Costain, what do you want?'

'Come on in and you'll find out.'

'You've nothing more to gain from me.'

'You figure wrong.' Costain's voice grew harsh. 'You quit stalling. Get in here or there's trouble for your daughters.'

Johnny knew the viciousness of the threat would bring Frank to the house. He must get out of sight and eliminate Ed Farnham. He moved stealthily but quickly up the remaining stairs. He crossed the landing towards the bedroom facing the front of the house. He flattened himself alongside the door which he was thankful to find slightly ajar. He hesitated. The slightest sound would bring suspicion, alarm and fatal consequence for the captives. To rush Farnham would give his presence away. Johnny drew his Colt then reached forward and gently pushed the door. It swung open slowly.

He heard a movement in the room then footsteps crossed the floor towards the door. Johnny tensed himself. Now it all depended on Farnham's reaction to the door's movement. Johnny banked on Farnham's curiosity being roused. He was right, Farnham reached the door and looked out. If he saw Johnny he got no chance to show his reaction for Johnny's Colt lashed down hard on his head. He started to pitch forward in unconsciousness but Johnny stepped forward quickly and supported him. The Hash Knife foreman turned the senseless Farnham, dragged him into the room and laid him on the floor.

Johnny moved to the window and took in the situation at one glance. Frank was nearing the house while Cap still sat on his horse about a hundred yards away.

Footsteps came along the corridor and crossed the hall to the front door. Johnny heard the door open and Costain's voice rip out an order harshly.

'Climb down and unfasten your gun belt.'

Johnny glanced down but Frank was hidden from his sight by the veranda awning sloping from the wall below the first storey windows. Now was his chance to let Cap know he was inside the house. He moved into full view close to the window. He waved. There was no reaction. He did not expect any extravagant movement from Cap which would alarm any watchers in the house, but some acknowledgement would reassure him that Cap could act with the knowledge that he was inside the house.

'Easy.' The warning came from Costain, and Johnny guessed Frank was in the process of loosening his gun belt. 'Drop it. Right, inside.' Johnny heard footsteps cross the veranda and enter the house. The door closed and the footsteps went to the room along the corridor. Johnny waved again and this time was relieved to see Cap make a slight movement with his right hand hanging loosely by his side. Cap knew. Johnny turned from the window and reached the top of the stairs just as Costain disappeared into the room and closed the door.

## THIRTEEN

Frank approached the house with only one thought in mind, saving his wife and daughters. He was still puzzled as to why Costain and Farnham had kidnapped them and were now holding him to ransom with their lives. What did they want? What more could they expect to get out of him? They'd got the ranch, the money from the drive, so what now? They'd probably know why Concho had followed him, could they know of Concho's end, expect him to be returning with the money and taking this way of getting the cash and avenging Concho? But how could they have heard of what happened at Moon Pass?

As he went into the house he realised he was in a tight corner. What could he hope to do to save them all? Cap would be under surveillance and the least sign that he was trying to intervene would doom them all. Johnny remained the only hope but from the back of the house how could he know what was happening, how could he do anything to help?

Frank's hopes were at a low ebb but he forced himself to keep alert, he must be ready to seize any half chance that offered itself.

They reached the room door and Costain indicated to him to open it.

Frank turned the knob, pushed the door open, stepped inside and pulled up short to stare in wide-eyed amazement at the man who stood, Colt in hand, grinning at him.

'Concho!' The word was sharp but hardly audible as it escaped from his lips.

'Frank!' Martha was across the room and into her husband's arms before anyone could stop her. 'Oh! Frank, what's this all about?' she cried. 'Out there he called you Wilkins.'

He held her tight and felt Cathy and Clare

hugging him while the tension and fear they had held under control broke down in a flood of tears.

'All right, it's all right,' whispered Frank, trying to reassure them. 'Jed Wilkins was my father.'

'Back off, ladies!' Concho's order was sharp, demanding instant obedience or take the consequences.

'Do as he says,' said Frank quietly. He was still surprised but he had got over the initial shock of seeing Concho, the man he had last seen swept by a foaming river over a waterfall in the mountains of Arkansas after being shot.

Martha put her arms round the girls' shoulders and gently led them away from their father.

'That's better,' approved Concho when they had reached the opposite side of the room. He grinned at Frank again. 'Didn't expect to see me again, did you?' Frank did not answer. Concho's face darkened with anger. 'Did you, Frank? Damn well answer when I ask a question!' His voice was shrill as he stepped menacingly towards Frank. Frank sensed Concho's tactics, humiliation in front of his family. All right, he didn't mind, he'd answer, that way he'd get more time which might provide a way out of their precarious situation at the hands of a man whose need for revenge was pushing him close to the limits.

'Course I didn't,' replied Frank.

'Thought I was dead, eh?'

Frank nodded. 'Last time I saw you you disappeared over that fall.'

'Yeah, but I got lucky. Plunged into a deep pool missing the rocks at the bottom of the fall. And my luck held as I was swept two hundred yards down stream. I made the bank, found the shot had taken me in the shoulder without doing any real damage. Found a small ranch, friendly rancher and his wife fixed me up. I figured you'd head for Cameron and I reckoned with luck I could outride you.' Concho grinned. 'I was right.'

'And what did it gain you?' said Frank.

'It let me fix a reception committee for you.'

'For what purpose?' Frank had guessed why and in it he saw a way to keep Concho talking. That he must do, for while part of his mind took in Concho's words the other half searched desperately for some way to save Martha and the girls.

Concho laughed harshly. 'Don't kid me, Frank. You know why. The money. I'd have it now if it hadn't been for that damned partner of yours. I thought I'd fooled you, figured you didn't know I was following you but all credit to you, you outsmarted me, having a partner to cover you. Lucky for me he wasn't a better shot.' Concho's eyes narrowed and darkened into a deep seriousness. 'Now let's quit the talking. I'll have the money.'

'I ain't got the money,' rapped Frank.

Anger smouldered in Concho's eyes. 'Don't play games with me Frank. You didn't go all the way to Arkansas and come back empty-handed.'

'I tell you I haven't got the money. You've got the ranch, the money from the herd, you've got the lot, I've nothing more to give so just let us go and you...'

Concho snarled. 'Frank for the last time...' He grabbed Cathy by the hair jerking her forward. The girl cried out with the sudden pain. Frank started but he could do nothing for Concho's cold Colt was pressing against Cathy's head.

Frank looked desperately at his wife. Bewilderment and fear for her daughter showed through the tears which filled her eyes. Anguish lined her face. Frank's heart went out to her. If only he could tell her what it was all about, relieve some of the hurt which was tearing at her. If they got out of this situation she would have to know, then their lives would lie in ruins. Whichever way he looked at it Frank realised this was the end, but whatever happened he must save Martha and the girls. Right now Cathy's death was near. Convincing Concho that he was telling the truth was not going to be easy.

'Frank, I don't know what this is all about but tell him for Cathy's sake!'

'Concho! Let the girl go!' Frank shouted.

'The money!'

'Let Cathy go and I'll talk.'

Concho hesitated, then suddenly released his grip on the girl's hair and at the same time pushed her roughly away. Cathy staggered and was only prevented from falling by her mother who held her tight while she wept.

'I'm waiting.' Concho's voice was cold with the hint of menace.

'Believe me, Concho, it's true, I haven't got the money.' The tone in Frank's voice made a desperate plea to be believed. He went on quickly before Concho could turn his threats once again to Cathy. 'That was no partner of mine that shot you. Remember Sheriff Nolan of Benton, well, somehow he got on to our trail. He shot you. I figured that was it as far as I was concerned, the sheriff had recovered the money and I faced a jail sentence but no, Nolan had other ideas. He was going to take the cash for himself and once again I faced being killed.'

'I suppose you're going to tell me your side-kick out there outwitted the sheriff,' mocked Concho.

'Right, he did,' put in Frank quickly. 'And then he persuaded me to return the money so he took it into Benton to the bank.' Frank was relieved that he had kept cool. It would have been so easy to have made a slip and mention Johnny but so long as Concho didn't know about him there was still a chance of escape.

Concho eyed Frank suspiciously for a moment then looked beyond him to Costain. 'Wade, bring that fella in.'

Wade nodded and left the room.

As he heard the room door opening, Johnny moved back quietly from the top of the stairs. He heard the footsteps come down the corridor and go to the front door.

'Get in here!' Costain shouted.

Johnny moved back to the top of the stairs

and saw Costain standing in the doorway with gun drawn, watching Cap approaching the house. Johnny was tense. He had to do something quick. Once Cap was in that room he would be completely on his own and it would be harder to effect a rescue.

Drawing his gun, Johnny moved stealthily down the stairs. He must reach Costain without Costain being aware of him. Gun shots out here could result in murder in the room. He reached the bottom of the stairs.

When Cap had seen Johnny move away from the window he held himself in readiness for any move which may be necessary as a result of Johnny's action in the house. It came as a surprise to him when the door opened and Costain appeared and called him into the house. His mind was toying with all the possibilities as he dismounted and walked towards the building.

Maybe Johnny had been caught. Maybe no opportunity to help Frank and his family had presented itself. In that case Johnny must still be in the house and aware that

Costain had come to the door. Maybe if he was able to hold Costain's attention Johnny might be able to do something.

'What do you want with me?' he called.

'You'll find out, just hurry it up,' snapped Costain.

'Frank Peters all right?'

'Quit the yapping.'

'Mrs Peters and the girls?'

'I said shut up and get in here.' Costain was annoyed at Cap's chatter.

But Johnny was delighted. It held Costain's attention. Johnny moved quietly towards the door. Costain started to turn so that Cap could pass him into the house. Cap saw Johnny and realised that if something wasn't done Costain would see Johnny. Cap stopped in his stride and started to turn away from the house. His movement had the desired effect. Surprised by Cap's action Costain stopped his own.

'Hi, what now? I said get in here.'

'Should have brought my horse and tied it up.'

'Forget it.' He stared hard at Cap. 'Ain't you the fella who rode with the Hash Knife foreman? Where is he?' His suspicions aroused Costain started to turn but those few moments, short though they were, gave Johnny just the time he needed. He was close to Costain before Costain felt his presence. Johnny's Colt slashed viciously across Costain's neck. He stumbled forward, jerked and Johnny's gun hit him again. Cap was at the veranda. He grabbed Costain and lowered him gently to the boards.

'Good work, Johnny,' he whispered.

'You too,' returned Johnny.

'Farnham's unconscious upstairs,' said Johnny.

'Then who's got Frank?'

'Third man, don't know who.'

'I'll take the window. You take the door. He'll be expecting me and Costain. When I see the door opening I'll take his attention by smashing the window.'

Johnny nodded and the two men moved away. Cap crept quietly along the veranda until he was beside the window. He could hear Johnny's footsteps echoing from the house. When he heard them stop he knew Johnny had reached the door. Cap peered cautiously into the room. He saw the door opening slowly. He reached forward and hit the glass pane sharply with the muzzle of his Colt.

The shattering glass startled Concho. He swung round at the sound and his gun blazed bullets at the window.

Almost at the same time Johnny hurled the door wide and in one swift glance took in the room. Frank was hurling himself at his family, desperately anxious to give them the protection of his body. Johnny squeezed the trigger. The room was filled with added explosion as his gun sent death streaking into Concho. He was punched backward by the impact. His eyes widened in amazement. He twisted as another bullet penetrated his body. Then his knees buckled and, as he pitched to the floor, his finger strengthened on the trigger and drove a bullet into the wood beneath his body.

Johnny stepped further into the room, his gun covering the still form. Footsteps echoed along the corridor and Cap rushed in. Three strides took him to Frank who was helping Martha and the girls to their feet. The two men hurried them from the room.

Johnny examined Concho. Satisfied that he was dead, he holstered his gun. He turned to follow the others when his attention was taken by a sheet of paper on the table. Glancing at it he saw that it was the document signed by Frank as he had handed over the ranch and the money from the sale of the cattle to Concho.

Johnny picked it up, folded it and slipped it into his pocket.

'Well, I should have done it years ago, Johnny. You and Cap were right about that. Martha said she hadn't married Sloane Wilkins but had married Frank Peters and they were different men. Shows how foolish it is to hide the past from someone you love.'

The two men were riding into Cameron while Cap had remained behind at the ranch.

'She says she'll move if we have to, she'll go with me wherever I want.'

'Maybe you won't have to,' said Johnny.

'That document I signed could still stand as legal,' commented Frank.

The two men reached Cameron, reported the shooting to the sheriff, who left for the Hash Knife with his deputy to see to the removal of the body and to take Costain and Farnham into custody.

Leaving the sheriff's office, Frank and Johnny crossed to the bank where they were greeted amiably by the manager. Without giving any information about his past, Frank told the bank manager about the signing of the document and about Concho's death.

'What I'd like to know,' he concluded, 'is where I stand now.'

The bank manager thought for a moment. 'I remember the document, two men brought it in to prove authorisation to claim the money from the sale of your cattle.

Know where it is now?'

'It will only prove that I signed everything to Concho Briggs.' Frank was dejected.

'Well,' mused the bank manager, 'I might be able to do something about that if I had the document.'

'In Frank's favour?' asked Johnny.

'Shan't know until I have it, but it's highly likely.'

Johnny felt in his pocket and produced the paper. 'It's right here.' As he handed it over to the bank manager he smiled at Frank's surprised look.

The bank manager took the piece of paper and without looking at it held it by one corner and applied the end of his cigar to the opposite corner until it burst into flames. The three men watched the flames climb the paper until the manager dropped it into a metal container for waste paper beside his desk. The remaining section flamed with a renewed brightness then subsided leaving only a brittle, black ash.

The bank manager stared at it for a

moment then muttered, 'Highly illegal, highly illegal.' He straightened with a smile. 'There you are, gentlemen. I figure a document signed under duress is better destroyed.'

'Thanks,' said Frank and his handshake expressed the depth of his gratitude.

'I take it you found that document at the Hash Knife,' commented Frank as he and Johnny rode back to the ranch, 'but why didn't you give it to the bank manager without all those questions?'

'To see if he favoured you. If he hadn't I'd have destroyed it and without it no one could have proved the Hash Knife wasn't yours.'

The publishers hope that this book has given you enjoyable reading. Large Print Books are especially designed to be as easy to see and hold as possible. If you wish a complete list of our books please ask at your local library or write directly to:

**Dales Large Print Books**
Magna House, Long Preston,
Skipton, North Yorkshire.
BD23 4ND